"Going somewhere?" Kane murmured

Kayla glanced up from buttoning her jeans. "I was just..."

"Leaving?"

"I thought a clean break would be best. You're going back to New Hampshire later today anyway, so I figured, this way, there would be no messy goodbyes."

Kane shook his head. Hadn't last night meant anything to her? Or did she just consider him a client? Either way, she'd gotten under his skin as no woman had done before. If anything could kill his edge, the one that kept him alert and alive, this was it. A soft, caring woman. Kayla Luck.

Kane drew a deep breath. It didn't matter why he'd come into her life. The fact remained that he'd compromised his principles, the case and his job. *Not bad for a night's work, McDermott.* But he still needed to know. Could it all have been one-sided?

He turned toward her, wallet open. "We never agreed on a price, but I'm sure this will cover last night's...lessons." He tossed the wad of bills onto the bed.

"What...is...that?" Kayla looked startled.

"You said we'd see how things went." He gestured toward the money. "That's payment for services rendered."

Dear Reader,

Sisters. Since I've never had one, I couldn't resist the opportunity to explore the bond between them and see what I missed! So in this two-alarm Blaze, you'll meet Kayla and Catherine Luck, sisters and best friends who *get very, very "lucky"*! In *Simply Sinful,* Kayla Luck has it all—brains, beauty and a body to make any centerfold jealous. But the men in her life had been unable to see beyond the packaging. Enter my dark, brooding hero, Kane McDermott. He's just the man to bring Kayla out of her shell and show her just how wonderful things between a man and a woman can be. There's just one problem—he's *Detective* Kane McDermott and he's investigating Kayla's business. How do love and trust overcome betrayal? Turn the pages and find out.

And don't forget to come back next month to follow sexy, spirited Catherine Luck's romantic adventures in *Simply Scandalous.* In the meantime, I'd love it if you could write and let me know if I'm making *your* reading fantasies come true: P.O. Box 483, Purchase, NY 10577. Or check out my web site at: http://www.eclectics.com/carlyphillips.

Happy reading,

Carly Phillips

Books by Carly Phillips

HARLEQUIN TEMPTATION
736—BRAZEN

SIMPLY SINFUL
Carly Phillips

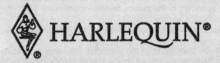

HARLEQUIN®

TORONTO • NEW YORK • LONDON
AMSTERDAM • PARIS • SYDNEY • HAMBURG
STOCKHOLM • ATHENS • TOKYO • MILAN • MADRID
PRAGUE • WARSAW • BUDAPEST • AUCKLAND

To Kathy Attalla, Janelle Denison and Shannon Short—
three wonderful friends who will undoubtedly run for
cover next time I say I'm writing a story with
intrigue elements. This one's for you!

ISBN 0-373-25875-5

SIMPLY SINFUL

Copyright © 2000 by Karen Drogin.

This edition published by arrangement with Harlequin Books S.A.

Visit us at www.romance.net

Printed in U.S.A.

1

LET HER BE CHARMED! Step inside and be transformed.

Kane McDermott peered through the space between the closed curtains in the brownstone's window. He got a brief glimpse of chin-length blond hair and a body with enough curves to make a centerfold jealous. It was a cold autumn day but the unexpected jolt of desire kicked in fast, warming him from within.

If he had to wine, dine and proposition her at least he wouldn't be bored. But he still resented the hell out of this assignment. Coming off a tough case, his superior thought he needed a rest. Captain Reid hadn't used the words burned out, but Kane heard them in the lectures anyway. He disagreed. Just because a drug bust had gone down wrong didn't mean he needed R&R. Having grown up on the Boston streets, he knew better than anyone when he was in danger of losing his edge. Now wasn't it.

He could wish to hell and back the wrong kid hadn't gotten hit in the crossfire but it wouldn't change the fact that he had. It wasn't Kane's bullet. The kid got taken down by his own brother. Logically, Kane knew it wasn't his fault, but that didn't lessen Kane's sense of guilt. Nor his remorse. Though no one could have anticipated the arrival of the dealer's little brother, Kane would live with the mother's screams for the rest of his life. He'd refused time off—he knew it wouldn't help him forget—so the captain figured Kane might as well pretend he'd taken leave.

Any rookie could verify whether Charmed! was a legitimate etiquette school for men or a front for a prostitution ring. Kane groaned aloud. As far as he was concerned, any guy who needed lessons in dating etiquette was as pathetic as this fluff assignment. What the hell kind of dork needed charm school to make headway with a woman? Especially one that looked like her.

He shook his head. What a waste. Then again, giving lessons to geeks was preferable to any other kind of service she might be performing for her paying customers. Considering she'd worked for her late aunt and uncle when they'd held the reins, she definitely knew the score. Whatever that was.

He might not know *her* agenda, but he knew his own—and this ridiculous case wasn't it. He'd pulled serious undercover work with drug dealers and pimps, yet here he was gearing up to make his awkward pitch to Charmed!'s sexy owner. He still had his doubts he could pull off the geek act and had a contingency plan in case he blundered. He wouldn't know until he got inside.

He placed his hand on the doorknob. The metal

was ice-cold from the cool spring air. Was she or wasn't she? It was time to find out.

KAYLA LUCK threw a disgusted glance at the old heater, which refused to cooperate with reasoning or common sense. Heat was unnecessary in the spring but the cleaning crew seemed to have forgotten. They'd turned the heater up last night and turned the brownstone into a sauna. Kayla had finally gotten the dial to move, but the darn thing continued to pump heat. Between the rising temperature and the effort she'd exerted trying to fix it, she was hot and uncomfortable. Definitely not the way to begin a new class, so she hoped all the men received the cancellation message.

Unable to take the layers sticking to her skin, she peeled off her jacket, leaving herself dressed in a silk shell and trousers. When that didn't help, she pulled at the light camisole that stuck to her skin. With a frustrated sigh, she glanced upward, at the bi-level unit she'd inherited along with the business.

While her sister Catherine's share of the inheritance had enabled her to fulfill her dream of going to culinary school, Kayla had put off her own dreams in favor of running the business and bringing in income. The old brownstone was quaint, offering two levels and too many rooms. For years, her aunt had run an old-fashioned service offering ballroom dancing and dating etiquette. There was a time when those kinds of services had been in demand, but the last decade had seen a steady decline in business.

Kayla had hoped to guide her aunt and help bring things out of the stone age. Her aunt had remarried last year and brought her new husband into the business. Kayla hadn't had a chance to broach the newlyweds about business changes. Her aunt and new uncle had died too soon.

Kayla intended to carry on anyway. Men today didn't need dating lessons but many executives required instruction on how to conduct themselves in social settings and learning foreign customs when entertaining international guests. With her language skills, she could add a modern dimension to an old-fashioned business. Ordering off foreign menus would no longer be a challenge for the American executive or traveler. And thanks to her well-targeted advertising, she'd just begun getting calls from the larger downtown corporations with offices overseas.

A far cry from the old-world charm school Charmed! had once been. Instead of giving *class to the heathens* as her aunt had been fond of saying, Charmed! would offer a broader, more modern range of services. When she'd inherited the school, the irony wasn't lost on Kayla. The class *bimbo* with the classless mother, giving *charm* lessons. The memories still hurt and gave her an even stronger incentive to upgrade and modernize Charmed! until it no longer resembled its roots.

Much as Kayla had done for herself. She'd grown up on the poor side of town in an otherwise well-to-do area outside of Boston. While the other kids always seemed to sport designer labels and the latest fashions, she and her sister had worn their clothes until they were threadbare. Problem was, Kayla's figure had developed early and her clothes never fit properly. The girls thought her a joke and the boys figured if she dressed in tight clothes, she wanted to be noticed. By the time she hit high school, there wasn't a guy who didn't claim he'd *gotten lucky*. She'd buried herself in her books and told no one except her sister the truth. No one else would have believed her if she had.

Despite the heat, she shivered at the painful memories, then forced them aside. Those days were behind her and Charmed! wasn't a joke. It wasn't a dating school for the awkward man. Not anymore. It was a legitimate business meeting legitimate needs. She wasn't thrilled with delaying her life, or putting off going back to school to obtain her language degrees. She'd even toyed with the idea of becoming an interpreter, but not at the expense of family. Charmed! was a family business and family was one of the few things Kayla and Catherine held sacred. Antiquated or not, neither she nor her sister had been ready to part with the school. Her aunt's sudden death two months earlier was too fresh and raw.

She grabbed for her pad and pen. The repairman still hadn't returned her call and she made a note to nudge him every half hour. She had a head for numbers, and the ability to memorize whole passages of books at a glance, but if she didn't record the little details in life, nothing got done.

Her projections indicated Charmed! would see a

large profit next year and she'd be able to stop renting the mirrored dance room out to exercise classes. She walked back to the storage room. With classes canceled, she could use the free time to begin going through her late aunt and uncle's books. But first she needed fresh air. She walked into the outer room, intending to open the doors and windows. Without warning, the chimes signaled that an unexpected visitor had entered. She glanced up and nearly tripped midstride.

She'd heard the expression sucker-punched before, but Kayla thought she and her wary heart were immune. Her visitor made her rethink that notion.

From his wing-tip shoes to his tawny and immaculately groomed hair, the man emanated strength and power cloaked in a double-breasted suit. Her breath caught in her chest. She was grateful she had been too hot and uncomfortable to eat because her stomach lurched in an unfamiliar combination of excitement, trepidation and awe. Heat settled over her in a huge wave that had nothing to do with the broken unit in the back.

She'd wanted to cool off? Not even the spring breeze blowing in behind him would cause her blood to chill now. At a professional glance he looked every inch the executive she wanted to target with her new business angle. From a personal standpoint, he set her body tingling with one long glance. "Can I help you?" she asked.

He nodded and offered an awkward smile. "Charmed?" He held out his hand, then seemed to reconsider, then changed his mind again and shoved his hand forward, nearly hitting her in the chest.

She tipped her head to the side, stunned by his awkward manner. "It's nice to meet you, too."

He laughed aloud, a sexy rumbling sound that vibrated inside her. A confident sound at odds with the inept handshake he'd offered. "No, I meant the sign outside said Charmed! so I assume I have the right place." The voice was every bit as sexy as the man.

A renewed surge of warmth trickled through her veins, slow and easy, like warm molasses. She liked the feeling. "That you do. I'm Kayla Luck, the owner." She shook his outstretched hand.

His touch was strong and self-assured, so unlike the weak handshake of the men she'd met at the accounting firm where she used to work.

"Glad to meet you, Ms. Luck." Without warning, he began pumping her hand too eagerly. "Or is it Mrs.?" He paused a beat. "I really should have asked, I mean I have no right to jump to conclusions and insult a lady..."

Unable to comprehend his sudden rambling, she interrupted him. "It's Ms. or Miss. Your choice. Personally I was never into feminist lingo." She eased her hand out of his grip before he yanked her arm out of its socket. The rough edges of his skin brushed against hers. Despite all logic, she enjoyed the lingering caress.

"No Mrs.," he mused. "Must be my 'lucky' day."

He shook his head and laughed. "That was pathetic. You must hear jokes like that all the time."

"Too often. What can I..." Kayla caught her slip. "I mean what can Charmed! do for you, Mr....?"

"McDermott. Kane McDermott."

"Are you here for the wine-tasting class, Mr. McDermott? Because it's been canceled."

He wiped the back of his hand across his forehead. "I can see why. It's a damn furnace in here."

"Actually it *is* the furnace."

"Which explains why you've stripped for summer before the start of the season." All traces of awkwardness gone, his smoky gaze fell on the silk shell that clung to her skin.

Embarrassment nearly suffocated her. She started to cross her arms and stopped, realizing she'd made a bad situation worse. She recognized the bold admiration in his chiseled features, the frank appraisal common to most men she'd come in contact with. Throughout her twenty-five years, she'd grown to both know and hate that stark, assessing look. Yet somehow, with his velvet stare boring into hers, she couldn't take offense.

Even so she couldn't possibly be interested in a stranger with too many inconsistencies in his character. Awkward one minute, self-assured the next, Kayla couldn't help but wonder who he was.

And what he wanted.

She darted a glance across the room. He might have been prepared to walk into a photo shoot instead of her place of business. His blond-streaked hair had been slicked back, the bottom curling around his collar as if fighting the stiff hold he'd tried to maintain. The cut was longer than most nine-to-fivers preferred and added a dangerous edge to his appearance. The hard look in his eyes seemed to verify that impression. The perfectly sculpted features were at odds with the man inside. Mr. Kane McDermott had been around life's many corners more than a few times.

He wasn't the ordinary man who frequented her aunt and uncle's establishment. *Her* establishment, she reminded herself. The man was a paying customer, and that meant she had to quit dissecting him and get down to business.

"Can I get you a cold drink?" she asked.

He leaned against the wall, one shoulder propped against the scarred wooden paneling. His potent gaze never strayed from hers. "How about I buy you a drink?" he asked in that seductive voice. "I mean...oh, hell. I can't pull this off."

"Pull what off? What's going on?"

"I can't pretend I'm a geek in need of training."

She raised an eyebrow. "You think that's the services we offer?"

"Let her be Charmed!?" he asked, repeating her aunt's company slogan. "It was on the pamphlet my friend gave me."

"I see. Well, we've advanced beyond those days. Not that we can't offer basic etiquette lessons if you need them, but... What do you mean you can't *pull this off*? That you can't *pretend* you're a geek in need of training?" she asked warily, steering the conversation back to her main concern. It wasn't like her to be sidetracked by a good-looking man—which made this one all the more dangerous.

"A friend of mine sent me here. He attended one of your dance classes last year. Your name is too unique for me to be mistaken."

She narrowed her gaze. "What's your friend's name?" Kayla asked.

"John Fredericks. Says he nearly flunked out of Ballroom Dancing."

She rolled her eyes, remembering the lessons her aunt had insisted Charmed! offer. Kayla never did understand how they filled a class. "That's because he had two left feet and was preoccupied with landing a date for New Year's Eve." She couldn't see the good-natured but shy man as a friend of Kane McDermott's, but apparently appearances were deceiving. If John and Kane were friends, Kane had just handed her a reference she could trust. "How is he?" she asked.

"His company sent him overseas. He said to ask your aunt for tips on dating French women," Kane said with a grin. "For the next time he calls."

Kayla felt a pang of regret. "She'd have been glad to give him advice. She liked John, too."

"What happened?" Kane asked.

"She and my uncle were killed a few months ago."

"Together?"

"Yes." Tears stung behind her eyes, as they did each time she thought of the accident and the aunt with whom she'd had so much in common. They shared an above-average IQ as well as a special relationship, due in large part to the fact that her aunt understood the oddity of being too smart.

She shook off the memories and focused on her visitor. "The police said they skidded in the rain and hit a tree."

"I'm sorry, that must have been rough...losing both of them at once."

"I didn't know my uncle well. They'd only been married a little over a year, but at least he made her happy before she—" Kayla stopped, realizing she was confiding in a total stranger.

"I'm sorry." He paused. "John will be sorry, too."

"Thank you." She lowered her gaze before meeting his stare once more. "But my aunt being gone doesn't change the facts."

"Which are?"

"You came in here pretending to be something you're not."

He flinched. "And that was wrong. But John...he thought we'd hit it off." He glanced down at his hands.

"Why didn't you just say that when you came in?"

"Because you can't trust someone else's opinion. Hell, that's like accepting a blind date. So I...came in here to check you out," he admitted sheepishly.

"John must have told you about me a long time ago," she said.

"Why's that?"

"Because Charmed! rarely offers classes for the

dating impaired anymore and neither does our brochure. We concentrate more on the international business arena now."

He had the grace and manners to look embarrassed. "I knew the minute I walked in here I couldn't pull it off," he muttered.

"So you said." Kayla narrowed her gaze. "Why is that?" she asked, hoping that her cup size had less to do with his answer than the chemistry. She was attracted to his looks, but a lot of good-looking men existed in the world. This one affected her on a deeper level.

"You're even more beautiful than I'd hoped."

A little too smooth, she thought with chagrin. So much for her futile hope he'd be special.

"But beyond that if you actually teach all these classes, there's a wealth of knowledge in there and, I'm not ashamed to admit, smart women turn me on," he said with a boyish grin.

Despite herself, she laughed at his obvious attempt at humor.

"Does this mean you'll go out with me?" he asked.

Oh, how she wanted to, but dating a stranger wasn't a smart move. She glanced at his determined gaze and doubted he'd take a straight no for an answer. "I wish I could, but I have to be here for the repairman." She forced a regretful smile and squelched the female buried inside her who wanted to accept his invitation.

He unbuttoned his suit and slipped the jacket off his broad shoulders before flinging it onto the nearest chair. "It was that or be roasted alive." He turned back to her. "Now where were we? Oh, yes...you going out with me."

She opened her mouth to insist she'd made her final decision when the phone rang. She picked it up, grateful to discover on the other end the plumber returning her call. Gratitude quickly turned to dismay. She placed the receiver back on the cradle.

Kane raised his dark eyebrows. "Problem?"

She nodded. "The repairman. He'll be here. Tomorrow. He hopes." She plucked at her damp shirt.

"Well then." He started to unbutton the cuff on his shirt. "We'd better get to work."

"We?" she asked.

"You and me. I don't see anyone else volunteering." His gaze darted around the room. "Do you?"

"No, but...are you a plumber?"

"No, ma'am. But living in an old apartment, I've seen my share of broken heaters. So let's get going." With a flip of his wrist, he began rolling up his sleeve. When the first one was finished, he began on the second, revealing muscular forearms and bronze skin. With her fair complexion, she always admired deep-olive skin, but his coloring had little to do with the pulse-pounding adrenaline flowing through her system.

It was one thing to sense this man's strength, another to witness the physical evidence of it firsthand. Kayla's mouth grew dry and she grabbed for the bottled water sitting on her desk. She wet her parched lips before attempting to speak. "Wrench?"

"What?"

She plucked up the tool she'd deposited on her desk earlier. "I asked if you needed a wrench. To shut off the heat."

"Take it along and we'll see."

She followed him into the back room. He knelt down to examine what she considered a foreign piece of equipment.

"The temperature's already turned down," he said.

"The cleaning crew must have turned it on by mistake. It was near ninety when I got here. I got the dial turned down but the heat didn't follow."

"It probably needs to hit its peak before it'll start coming down."

"You mean it's going to get hotter?" she asked, fingering the damp bangs that stuck to her forehead.

"Count on it." His searing gaze zeroed in on hers and the heat in the room seemed to soar. No man had ever had such a heart-stopping effect on her before. Drawing a deep breath, she wondered how to handle such raw masculinity. She'd made too many mistakes to mess up again.

He cleared his throat. "There's another choice. We can hit the emergency switch and hope we don't blow the unit in the process."

She shook her head. "No, thank you. Can't afford *that* kind of repair."

"Then you have no choice but to let it run its course. In the meantime, do you have a bucket?" he asked.

"As a matter of fact..." She retrieved the pail her aunt had used to store cleaning supplies. "Here." She offered it and he grabbed the handle.

"What about a skate key?" he asked.

She blinked at the strange question. "A what?"

He chuckled. "Never mind." He reached around and patted the floor surrounding the heater. "Aha." He held a small rounded key aloft. Triumph lit eyes that she now realized were stunning—an aqua mix that emphasized more blue than green and turned her already mixed up insides to pure mush.

She glanced at his find. "Let me guess. A skate key?"

"Sort of. Most of these old units need to be bled at the start of every season, sometimes more often. People familiar with them leave the key in a place they won't forget. Otherwise you have to go running and hope you can find..."

"The nearest skater?" she asked wryly.

"She'd do in a pinch...if she looked like you."

A burning flush heated her cheeks. Thanks to her fair skin she probably resembled a tomato by now. "Look, Mr. McDermott, I appreciate your help, but you don't have to flatter me."

"Do compliments make you uncomfortable, Miss Luck?"

She shrugged, knowing he'd hit a nerve. In her experience, compliments were a means to an end.

"A woman like you should be used to them. I would think you'd take them in stride."

"Let's just say, I'd rather get back to the problem at

hand," she said, gesturing toward the heater. "I thought you bled a heater when there was no heat."

"You do. But you might as well stabilize the system so you don't have major problems when you turn it on again next winter." He turned back to the heater and soon the sound of water running into the bucket filled the otherwise silent room. After her third trip to empty the water into the bathroom sink, he flipped the key and rose to his feet.

"All set." He wiped his damp hands on his pants, unconcerned with the damage he did to his suit. "As for the unit, give it some time. Chances are it'll cool off without the help of the repairman."

"Just clueing me in might have saved me a small fortune. Thanks."

"Not a problem." His gaze bored into hers and a flash of dizziness assaulted her. She only wished she could blame the heat, but knew it was his penetrating stare that unnerved her.

"Reconsider that drink?" he asked.

She started to shake her head. "I..."

"Then I want lessons. And before you say anything, I know you don't specialize in dating etiquette anymore, but consider this an emergency. I have dinner with my boss tomorrow night and he plans on bringing his daughter. I don't want to get involved, but I'd like to make a good impression and bow out gracefully at the end. Dinner tonight so you can teach me the finer points of charm and class." He grinned and she discovered one dimple in his left cheek.

"I think you have enough of both," she said wryly.

"So humor me. I'm giving you an excuse to say yes...and you know you want to." His voice lowered an octave. Husky and seductive, it flowed through her veins.

"And I think you're taking a lot for granted. How about I make some calls and see if one of my instructors is available to, uh, meet your needs." She groaned inwardly. It had taken years to learn how to cover her insecurities, but Kayla had managed. Yet around Kane McDermott, she became the awkward girl she'd once been.

"I'd rather go with you." His intense gaze begged her to believe.

Could he possibly be interested in her? She shook her head.

"Too bad for me." Disappointment tinged his voice and dulled his gaze. He pointed to the phone. "Guess I'll be going with a stranger tonight."

She rolled her eyes. "*I'm* a stranger."

"Funny, but it doesn't feel that way." His gaze locked with hers in a meaningful stare she couldn't escape or mistake. There was a connection between them. They both knew it—just as they both knew he'd just changed her mind.

She lowered herself into the swivel chair behind her desk. Leaning across the wooden top, Kane came within kissing breadth of her lips and she caught an enticing hint of spearmint on his breath. "Are you going to disappoint a customer, Miss Luck?"

"Kayla." She licked her dry lips.

He raised an eyebrow and straightened to his full height. "It seems I've made progress, *Kayla*."

He most definitely had. "Well, I can't very well accompany you if you're going to call me Miss Luck all night," she said.

The flash of white teeth came and went in a quick grin. "I heard about this casual place. I forget the name." He buttoned his suit jacket. "I'm from out of town, so I'm not too familiar with the city. I expect to be visiting often, though, because the boss lives here." His gaze never left hers.

"So it's casual dinner?" she asked.

"Yes. You can run through wine ordering, dinner choices, all the necessary things I'd need to know for dinner with the boss...and I get your company. Like baseball?"

She nodded, feeling a little like she'd been blindsided.

"I've got tickets for the Red Sox game afterward and we can hit that later."

"Somehow I doubt you need lessons on how to attend a ball game."

"No, but by then I'm hoping we'll be past the lesson stage. Sound good?"

She cleared her throat. "Sounds fine." So fine it scared her.

"We're all set then."

She nodded.

"You won't be disappointed." His words held a wealth of meaning and Kayla had the distinct impression this was more than a business. That *she* was more than hired help to this extremely sexy man.

He reached out and grabbed her hand. The connection was instant, the knowledge frightening. She feared her deepest thoughts had just been confirmed. He jerked back without warning. Had he experienced the same unnerving reaction as she?

He reached into his pocket and withdrew a brown leather wallet, working quickly, as if he suddenly couldn't wait to be gone. "Do you take American Express or Visa?" he asked.

"Either, but..." What could she say? That the thought of taking money in exchange for an evening in his company seemed wrong?

She glanced at Kane. He'd charmed her despite his initial pretense. Not only did she like him but she could use an evening out to enjoy herself. With the all-business attitude she'd had lately, she'd barely had time for fun. When was the last time she'd been out with a nice guy? The last time she'd let herself *be* charmed for once? Kane was most definitely good at that. She bit down on her lower lip and met his gaze, which had darkened to an unreadable, darker blue.

He flipped open his wallet. "I can pay cash if you'd prefer."

"No." She couldn't take money in exchange for a date. No matter how he couched the word, that's what it was. She treated him to a genuine smile. "Why don't we see how things go and we can discuss it? Later."

"Okay." He snapped closed the billfold. "I'm staying at the Summit Hotel and I'll be in touch, Miss...Kayla." With a grin, he walked out the door, leaving her to wonder...

Could she really be that...lucky?

2

"YOU LOOK SHARP, McDermott." Whistles and cat-calls followed his walk through the station house. Kane ignored the harassment and parked himself in an open chair, kicking his legs out in front of him. He exhaled deep and easy, keeping up a steady beat. Relaxation came, but it was hard-won and destined not to last.

He'd taken one look at that angel-like face and known the geek cover wouldn't work. He'd given it a shot anyway...because it would have been a hell of a lot easier to keep his distance from the woman if he wasn't acting like himself. He was a professional. Attraction was never supposed to come into play.

Kane let out a groan. But he'd never seen eyes so wide-set and green and he'd damn sure never seen curves like hers anywhere but on a magazine center-fold. Desire hadn't hit him so hard or fast since he'd been a teenager.

"Well? Did the McDermott charm do her in?"

At the sound of the commanding voice, Kane lifted his gaze. Since he'd been pulled into the assignment last minute, he hadn't had a chance to go over his cover with Reid. Kane was grateful. He'd never live it down if the captain thought he'd gone in acting like a pencil-pushing geek. "She didn't say no, if that's what you're asking. You get the tickets?"

Reid ran a hand over his balding head. "You're a pain in the ass, McDermott. Yeah, I called my brother-in-law and told him my best detective was into bribery now."

Kane shrugged. "Like I had a choice? Besides you're the one who insisted I take some R&R."

Reid's face grew somber. "Don't try to con me, McDermott. I've known you since you were a wise guy in the academy. You watch a kid get killed and you tell me you don't need R&R?" Reid snorted. "I haven't seen you so shaken since your first shot actually hit its target."

Kane didn't reply. The captain was right. When he was a rookie, Kane had fatally wounded a suspect when he'd closed a drug bust. The captain had picked Kane up and taken him home afterward, and, since then, the Reids had become the family Kane insisted he didn't need.

The captain knew him well. More importantly, he had accepted him. Despite Kane's surly attitude and attempts to remain aloof, Reid pushed anyway, including him on holidays and family gatherings. After a while, the older man's persistence had paid off. Kane couldn't bring himself to insult Reid or his wife by turning them down, though he squelched the small part of him that wanted to enjoy the sense of family they provided. Kane limited the occasions, but he still knew the Reid clan better than he knew anyone else.

"At least these tickets will work to our advantage," Reid said in his raspy voice.

"You really ought to lay off the smokes, Captain."

Reid scowled at him. "Worried I won't be around to bug you?" He laughed. "I'm too tough to die."

"You got that right," Kane muttered, refusing to admit he cared too much about his boss.

"Thanks to the predicted drop in temperature, the lady should be more than eager to share body heat," he said, ignoring Kane as usual. "She seem interested?"

Kane folded his arms behind his head and leaned back to ponder the question. The old chair and springs creaked beneath his weight in a familiar song. *Had* Kayla Luck been interested?

"More after I told her I knew Fredericks." Their tip regarding Charmed! had come from a reliable source—an up-and-coming politician who'd gotten caught with his pants down. He'd been more than willing to talk in exchange for keeping his escapade out of the headlines.

Reid had gotten a list of Charmed!'s *legitimate* clientele over the past year. Fredericks seemed squeaky-clean and nervous to have his name tainted by scandal. Kane hadn't trusted the guy to keep quiet should Kayla contact him about his salesman friend, Kane McDermott, so he'd concocted the story about Fredericks being transferred overseas. Fredericks had been jumpy but sincere and he'd sung Kayla Luck's charms, including her honesty.

"At least you picked a winner out of the hat."

Kane nodded in agreement. If Kayla had reacted badly to the name, the plan would have been shot to hell. "I'm good at what I do. Think she'll take the bait?"

Kane recalled the sultry smile, the soft pout of her lips and the coyly phrased question. *Why don't we see how things go?* "Yes...and no." She'd been interested, all right. The thought caused a steady, pulsing rhythm in his veins. But he could deal with a sexual attraction. Lust and desire were two sensations he could easily handle.

The lady's other qualities were another story. A naive innocence lurked beneath the seductive body. She lacked the hard edge he'd expected, the tough facade he'd been prepared to face. Instead she'd been uncertain and unsure. She might have grown up on the wrong side of the tracks, but life hadn't visibly hardened her, at least not yet.

Lush curves on the outside and a gentleness on the inside. It was the softness that beckoned to him and that shook him up.

"Either the lady's running more than a charm school or she isn't," the Captain said.

Kane shrugged, recalling her uneasiness at dealing with compliments and her unwillingness to accept his initial invitation. An act? A game designed to bait a man, to entice him until they fell into a sweaty tangle between the sheets? Or the ultimate rarity on this planet, an honest soul with nothing to hide? Kane had no idea.

"We'll see."

Captain Reid smacked his hand on the metal desk. "No, *you'll* see, McDermott. Just make sure you pay more attention to the lady than you do to the game."

Kane didn't take offense. The old man's gruff ways had kept Kane going too many times, when he'd watched neighborhood friends overdose or go down on a bust. The older man had faith in a young kid even when no one else cared enough to bother. He knew Kane's sense of duty was strong.

"After this one I don't want to see your sorry butt in here until the middle of next week."

"A good weekend to you, too. Say hi to Marge."

"Do it yourself," Reid grumbled. "She says you don't come by often enough." He turned and strode back into his office.

Kane got his mind back on the case. He let the captain's words about Kayla sink in. Doling out attention to Ms. Luck wouldn't be a hardship. In her silk top and pearl earrings she was a sexy woman who any guy would be lucky to claim as his own.

Except a cop whose job it was to take down a prostitution ring...if it existed. Her place could be a front as his informant claimed. Maybe the sister knew more than Kayla, but according to his files, Catherine Luck had signed over ownership and was more concerned with her education than the school that paid for it.

He swiveled back and forth in his seat. He had a hard time believing the innocence in that green-eyed gaze wasn't real but an act for the customer's benefit.

His hands clenched into fists at the thought of Miss Kayla Luck.

Chemistry flared between them hot and strong. Unmistakable. Verbal seduction wouldn't be a problem tonight, but keeping his hands to himself just might be. He shook his head, trying to dislodge any thoughts caused more by emotion than common sense. Cash in exchange for sex, he reminded himself. Money up-front. Stick to the plan and the answers would follow.

And Kane always stuck to the plan. As a punk-kid, he'd followed a different code of conduct than the one he lived by now, but respecting the law on the street had kept him alive. As a cop, he walked on the other side. The rules were different but the reasoning the same. If he followed the rules, he kept his edge honed. Anything less and he didn't deserve his badge.

Kane closed his eyes and a vision of Kayla danced before them. Between a body made for a man's touch and a heart-shaped face that would test a saint, he had the distinct notion he needed that edge more than ever before.

"IT'S A BASEBALL GAME, not a formal banquet."

"It's a date, not order-in Chinese food with your sister," Catherine countered. She threw a disgusted glance at Kayla's old sweatshirt and blue jeans. "Are you trying to turn the man off before he gets to know how disgustingly smart you are?"

Kayla thought back to his references about her

classes and how *smart women turned him on*. He couldn't possibly know that much about her after such a brief meeting. It had to be a lucky guess. "I don't want to look too eager," she said.

"More like you don't want to look too easy." Her sister grabbed Kayla's hand. Head held high, Catherine led the way to her bedroom, a short distance down the hall from Kayla's own. With dramatic flair so opposite to Kayla's more subdued actions, Catherine flung open the closet door and began riffling through the clothes inside.

"They won't fit," Kayla muttered.

"Maybe we don't share the same bra size, but don't tell me you don't steal my clothes every once in a while."

"Borrow."

"What's the difference?" Catherine held up a yellow blouse, made a face and hung it back on the rack. "I know I swipe yours." She came out of the small walk-in with a white turtleneck and a pale blue satin jacket. "Here. Leave the jeans and try this. The jacket's quilted, by the way. It's supposed to be chilly tonight."

Kayla glanced at the outfit, more casual than her usual Brooks-Brothers type look. Still, when she tried on the clothes, she had to admit she looked okay. Catherine made a show of walking around her twice, hands on her hips in a judgmental pose. "Perfect. Better than all those trousers and silk blouses you wear. So stuffy—even Mama wouldn't have left the house like that."

"Mama liked to dress her own way," Kayla said, thinking of the woman who had raised her girls alone. A woman with a heart of gold, but tarnished luck.

They hadn't had much money, but their mother had always made sure she looked her best before leaving the house. Unfortunately *her best* too often fell short. She looked like what she was: the checkout girl at the local supermarket, an aging woman still attempting to look younger than her years. Until Catherine had taken over clothes shopping, the Luck sisters had usually gone to school looking like mini-clones of their beautiful, but flamboyant mother.

"Men definitely took notice," Catherine said.

"Too bad she never looked at them. Maybe things would have been different."

"Maybe Mama wouldn't have died of overwork and a broken heart?" Catherine shook her head. "She chose her life."

"She liked pining for Daddy, that's for sure. You ever wonder if Daddy pined back?" Kayla asked.

Her sister shook her head. "I think one kid scared him to death, two made him worse than a coward."

"Do you really have to sound so...full of hate?" Kayla muttered.

"I don't hate him. Actually I don't feel much about him at all. But truth is truth." Catherine pinned her with her steady gaze. "I don't think all men are like him if that's what you're thinking."

"Not in the love 'em and leave 'em department," Kayla agreed. "But in the can't keep their hands to themselves department, men are all the same." After all, her parents had had Kayla and Catherine within one year of each other. If that wasn't a prime example of too much lovin', as her mother liked to call it, then she didn't know what was.

Catherine lowered herself onto her frilly white bedspread. "You know, a guy not keeping his hands to himself can be nice."

For someone with Catherine's confidence, maybe. Kayla joined her, staring at her fingers spread over her jean-clad legs. "Are you going out tonight?" Kayla asked.

"You bet. Dancing at Shooters." She snapped her hands in the air. "With Nick."

Nick had been Catherine's best friend for years. Kayla suspected he'd once been in love with her beautiful sister, too. But Cat wasn't interested and Nick had moved on, apparently content as Cat's best friend. And Catherine was alone.

Kayla narrowed her eyes and took in her sister's miniskirt and tights, her stretch top that showed off delicate curves. Catherine didn't have Kayla's lush figure, but she attracted her own share of attention. Kayla admired her sister but she also knew she had her own share of insecurities. Cat covered them well but the truth was obvious. Both Luck sisters had been scarred by their childhood experiences.

Each Luck sister had reacted in a different way. Instead of becoming a social butterfly, Kayla had learned to push men away. Although she had a lingering desire for hearth, home and a white picket fence, she knew better than to believe she'd find it or the perfect man to share her life with.

Catherine placed a sisterly hand over hers. "Maybe you've never found the right guy. The one who will put *you* first."

"You think he exists?" Kayla asked but Kane immediately came to mind. He was the one man she didn't want to push away physically or turn off emotionally. He was the first guy who made her feel special, who made her want to take chances.

Catherine shrugged. "I don't know. But if the light in your eyes is any indication, you do. And I'd hate to see you lose that special someone out of fear."

She grinned. "He was different and sexy and..."

"And?"

"He listened," she said, somewhat embarrassed. "He was interested, if I'm not mistaken, but I've been out of the game too long to know for sure."

Catherine shook her head. "You don't need experience to know if he makes you feel special. This guy could be *it*."

Kayla had the sense that Kane was most definitely *it*. "I don't really know him," Kayla reminded her sister.

"But you want to." Catherine read her mind as she had so many times in the past. "And just wait until he gets a look at you tonight." Walking back to the closet, Catherine reached inside and tossed something across the room.

Kayla stood before the full-length mirror behind the door. She spun around once more, shocked at the woman whose reflection she saw there. "I don't even recognize myself," she said, as she added the finishing touch, a wide headband that would provide both warmth and style for the night ahead.

"That's because you've been so busy hiding behind conservative clothes and a job that involves geeks not hunks. You've just forgotten there's a woman inside."

Was Catherine right? Of course she was. Between her old accounting job and now running her aunt's business, Kayla had stifled her sense of self. Add to that her self-imposed lack of a love life and things seemed pretty pathetic about now.

Her sister placed her hands on Kayla's shoulders. "At least this guy has brought my sexy sister out of her shell." Catherine grinned.

"He's a customer," Kayla said. As if that meant anything. As he'd said, the customer thing was an excuse to let her say yes to a date without thinking too much. It was eerie how well Kane McDermott had understood her.

"Since when do you date a *customer?*"

She met Catherine's gaze in the mirror. "I don't," she admitted.

"I know. And that's why I think you should go out and *feel* for once. Take things from there." Catherine plucked at the headband, straightening it to look suitably stylish. "The clothes are just the trappings of freedom. The rest is up to you."

Catherine turned her toward the door to the bedroom and steered her into the hall. "I'll drop you off

at the restaurant. It's on my way and, besides, I want
to get a look at this guy firsthand."

"Checking him out, Mom?"

Catherine shrugged. "We've always looked out
for each other. No sense stopping now." She glanced
at Kayla. "You think about what I said. You might
live to regret it if you don't."

Kayla took her sister's advice, all the way to the
outside of the restaurant. He'd given her directions
to it during their brief phone conversation and Catherine had given her a lift. Kane waited on the top
step, his elbow resting on the brass railing. Irre-
sistible in a black leather jacket, he could show her
his charms anywhere, anyplace, anytime, she decided.

Catherine's whistle brought Kayla back down to
earth.

"I take it you approve?"

Catherine answered with a grin. Kayla finger-
combed her hair and stepped out of the car. Kane
was by her side in an instant. During the brief intro-
ductions and small chitchat between Kane and Catherine, Kayla could barely concentrate.

Was her sister right? Was this man, this date, a
not-to-be-missed opportunity? Could he be someone
in her future? Kayla wasn't sure, but she was about
to find out. And who deserved an honest chance
more than Kane McDermott, the first man to excite
her and impress her?

The first man to look past her appearance and who
genuinely seemed to like the woman within.

WITH HIS HAND ON her back, Kane steered Kayla out of Fenway Park and into the dimly lit Boston streets. The Sox had won in extra innings and the woman beside him hadn't uttered a single complaint about sitting through the long game or the continuing drop in temperature. Under ordinary circumstances, he'd call the date a hit, but Kayla was no ordinary woman, any more than she was his real date, a fact he had to keep reminding himself of time and again.

"Did I tell you I loved that restaurant?" she asked.

Only about ten times, he thought, wondering why the hell the notion pleased him so much. "The meal or the atmosphere?" he asked.

She laughed, the sound doing more to warm him than his heavy leather jacket. "Both. Wall-to-wall books..." She spread her arms wide, knocking into the people emptying out of the stadium along with them. "Oops."

Her laughter was contagious, her love of something as simple as books, refreshing.

"But who would have thought of turning a library into a restaurant, and keeping the old volumes on the shelves? How have I lived here for so long and never even known about that place? Where did you find it?"

"I have my sources," he said, deliberately vague.

"Well, tell them they were right on target." She laughed again and this time his stomach twisted with regret. Careful research and discreet questions into her background had revealed the blond bombshell was also an intellectual, a Phi Beta Kappa who hit the library most nights after work. Reading was obviously a hobby of hers, one he'd taken advantage of tonight.

The stab of guilt took him by surprise. His job had never bothered him before and it shouldn't now. As part of his assignment, he could just as easily clear her as convict her. Big deal if he had to dig deep and personal in order to accomplish his goal. But one glance into those trusting eyes turned him inside out. She wouldn't appreciate the lie. If she was guilty of running a prostitution service, he shouldn't give a good goddamn. But he did and the guilt stemmed less from sensing she wasn't involved and more from caring what she thought of him. That in itself was a first and Kane didn't like it a bit.

After an evening in her company, he'd learned plenty. This was a woman who cared about family, felt things deeply and had put her dreams on hold for her sister's future and out of respect for her late aunt. The innocence she projected in both her gaze and her gestures told him more than surveillance ever could and that innocence spoke to him. Touched him in ways no one ever had, in places he never allowed anyone to reach.

His gut told him she wasn't involved in anything more than running an inherited business. One she at times enjoyed, at others resented. Since gut instinct wasn't admissible in a court of law, he had to rely on his other talents to clear Miss Kayla Luck. Somehow proving her not guilty had taken precedence over making a case against Charmed!'s sensual owner.

"Don't ask me why, but I had a feeling you would like that place," he told her.

"You were right."

"I know." Because he was a man who prided himself on instinct. Research may have provided the background, but an hour in her company and Kane had discovered even more. All pretense of schooling forgotten, Kayla had opened up to him. He now knew her father's abandonment had left her hurt and wounded even if she didn't show it, and the mother she loved had been more a child than a useful, guiding parent.

Kayla had grown up on her own...like him. She had few close ties, apart from her sister...also like him. And by the time dinner ended, he knew how to reach her. He knew when to flatter and when to back off. He even knew how to make her feel beautiful without ogling, because the slightest show of male interest in her looks led to a hasty retreat. He had the sense he *knew* Kayla Luck. He had connected with her apart from his assignment and the thought made him too damn nervous.

As they rounded the next corner and walked down a street nestled between a double row of buildings, a heavy breeze whipped around them and the temperature seemed to drop even further.

He rubbed his hands together. "I'd kill for a..."

"Cup of hot chocolate covered with whipped cream," Kayla said, finishing his sentence but not the way he'd intended. Scotch or whiskey was what he'd had in mind. Something that burned like hell and shocked his system into remembering he was on assignment and not out with an intelligent, sexy woman. One he wanted to see again and not behind prison walls. And *that* wouldn't be happening.

He needed solid proof to take back to Reid. Time to make his move and get out, Kane thought. They'd both be better off.

He'd gotten nowhere with his subtle questioning earlier, which meant he'd have to take a more direct, a more *seductive*, approach. He dreaded the idea as much as his overheated body craved it. Not even the sharp wind biting at his face and reaching into his bones numbed the burning heat she aroused inside him.

"I was thinking more along the lines of coffee," he muttered. "But anything hot will do."

"No kidding." She nodded in agreement and clutched at her forearms with her hands. She was obviously cold but had no intention of voicing a complaint. Definitely a woman after his own heart. *No*, he contradicted himself, *not his heart*. That he'd walled off years ago. He'd learned early on if he made anything other than his job his priority, he risked losing the edge.

As a self-reliant kid, he'd honed the instincts that kept him alive. His uncle had agreed to take him in on the condition he made himself scarce. Kane had only swallowed his pride and asked for a place to crash in order to avoid social services and foster care. Basic survival was what Kane understood best. Sex fell under that heading, caring did not.

But he had a job to do. Time to stop stalling and find out, he thought. She was cold? The least he could do was warm up the lady. He looked down and her gaze connected with his. Wide-set eyes stared back and golden strands of windblown hair touched her reddened cheeks. Intense need kicked in strong. He had to taste her. That it might make or break his case had nothing to do with the fierce hunger lashing through him. He cupped his hands over hers, feeling the ice-cold of her skin and he drew her back into a hidden alley.

The crowds rushed past them, unconcerned with anything except finding warmth. Kane understood that need. He ran his hands up and down her arms. A tremor shook her and instinctively he knew it had nothing to do with the outside temperature and everything to do with body heat. His and hers.

One step and he'd backed her against a dark brick building. Desire rushed through him the moment his body came into contact with hers. Layers of clothing didn't matter, nothing mattered.

"Kane?"

He looked into questioning eyes and had no answers. None he could reveal to her and, worse, none he understood himself. Which suited him fine. He didn't need to understand; he needed to feel. Her lips on his, her body, slick and wet, molding around him, producing friction so intense it was unbearable. Not that he'd compromise his job. He wouldn't let things get that far, or if the informant was right, Kayla wouldn't, either, not without payment.

Looking into those trusting eyes, he damn well knew if she called a stop tonight, it would have nothing to do with money. This woman was no prostitute but he needed proof and to get it, he had to carry things through. One sampling of those full lips and he could attempt to close the deal. Once she backed off, he'd make some excuse and take her home. A cold shower waited for him and then he'd file his report and forget all about Miss Kayla Luck.

Plan set, he focused his attention on his so-called date, a woman who intrigued him more with each passing second. His grip on her arms tightened. She didn't protest, not when he pulled her toward him and not when his lips came down hard on hers. That was the point Kane knew he'd made a mistake. Her mouth was warm and welcoming and a hint of sweet wine still lingered inside. One taste made him hungry for more than a stolen kiss in a back alley. One sampling set his blood on fire and he knew: he wouldn't be walking away anytime soon.

The brick wall anchored them and he took advantage letting his body thrust hard against hers. She made a sound, half moan, half plea, Kane couldn't be sure. He only knew it made him want her more. The pulsing, pounding waves wouldn't be ignored.

Kayla leaned her head back against the wall, drawing deep unsteady breaths. He cupped her chin in his hand and looked into glazed green eyes. *He wanted her*. There it was. The stark truth, he thought. No lies, no deception, no *case* hanging between them...unless something she did placed it there. He'd crossed the line and there was no turning back.

He'd never have believed he'd be so tempted to compromise his principles for a woman, never have believed he needed one night so badly. She aroused him beyond sanity, beyond reason and he needed to possess her, all of her. He traced the line of her jaw, then held her face between his palms. "I want you." His voice rasped in his ear, the words vibrating between them.

Her hands reached for his chest, curling into fists against the heavy jacket. "Why?"

Of all possible answers, that one took him by surprise. So did the fact that he knew exactly what to say. "Not because you're beautiful, even though you are."

Her cheeks turned a shade deeper than before and he brushed his thumb over her reddened skin. She trembled and the shudder found an answer inside him. He inhaled then forced himself to continue. "And not because your body would tempt a saint, even though it would." His other hand brushed the underside of her breast, tracing the rounded, full contours hidden beneath the layers of clothes. Her answer, a sensual moan, shook his soul. For as he spoke, Kane realized he was telling her more than what she wanted to hear. He was telling her the truth.

She tipped her head to the side. Her face fit perfectly in his hand. "Then why?" she asked.

"Because you're smart and I respect that, because

you're gutsy and I admire that." Her eyes sparkled, glowing with a life of their own at each word he spoke.

Kane shook his head, unable to believe he was taking everything he'd learned about Kayla in order to make his case, and using it to make her his instead.

One night. With every second that passed, he needed that more and more. The light in her eyes, the...acceptance, he thought, struggling for the correct word. He needed everything she possessed. After taking it, he'd deal with how badly he betrayed both his job and himself. "I had fun with you tonight and everything about you intrigues me. Enough?" he asked too harshly.

A satisfied smile caught hold of her lips. He wanted a taste of that satisfaction but refrained for now. "More than enough." Her arms slipped around his waist.

"I take it that's a yes." His heart beat faster at the thought.

"That's a yes...for the right price," she said coyly.

He froze in place, then forced a smile. He'd taken her out tonight to bait and trap her. He'd gotten temporarily distracted by a rush of hormones, but it seemed he was about to get what he came for. He ignored the swell of disappointment that came when he looked into those fraudulent green eyes. "And what would that be, Ms. Luck?"

She touched her icicle-like hands to his face and grinned. "Hot chocolate, Kane." She smoothed her fingertips over his brow and her light laughter caught him by surprise. "What did you *think* I wanted?" she asked.

"I don't know, but you could show me."

Her eyes opened wide before she brushed a warm yet hesitant kiss over his lips. Arousal hit as fast as his sense of relief. Before he could change his mind, he grabbed her hand and started back down the street. His hotel room, the hotel room taken by the department, was a few blocks away. He'd face himself and the repercussions of his actions tomorrow. Tonight was about Kayla.

3

KAYLA WALKED INTO THE recently decorated lobby of
the hotel where Kane was staying, trying not to feel
like a woman about to embark on a one-night stand.
She glanced around at the potted, but obviously fake
plants and the bored clerk yawning behind the desk.
It was a respectable establishment, but she wondered how many men brought women to a hotel
room for a quick fling?

She stopped halfway to the elevator and grabbed
the hard leather of Kane's jacket. He turned toward
her. "Second thoughts?" he asked.

"Just a reality check. I don't know anything about
you."

"You know what's important." He brushed a fin-
gertip down her cheek. Her skin tingled and her
heart rate soared. "What more is there?" he asked.

"I don't know, maybe you're not really a salesman. Maybe you're a..."

"Serial killer?" He jumped in with a disarming
grin.

"Married or involved was more like what I had in
mind," she said on a nervous laugh. "But yours is a
valid consideration, too."

"Well, I can set your mind at ease on that score. No

bodies buried anywhere in my past. No spouses, either, present, ex or intended." He wrapped a comforting arm around her shoulder. Well, it would have been comforting if not for her body's immediate reaction.

Pheromones, she'd read recently, acted to stimulate a body's chemical reaction to the opposite sex. But such clinical reasoning wasn't enough of an explanation for her response to Kane McDermott. It might explain the all-over heat despite the chill outdoors, or the delicious sizzling sensations tripping around inside her. In no way did it account for the rush of warmth when those eyes met hers or the understanding she'd seen there when she'd told him about her childhood.

If he'd been vague about himself, that was okay. He'd be gone too soon for it to matter and he'd shown interest in her life, something no man had ever done before. His curiosity about her new career path and the new services she planned for Charmed! made her feel as if he cared.

Catherine was right. This was a man capable of putting Kayla and her needs first. But she'd never done anything like this before and she needed his reassurance before deciding to take this next step. She needed to know there was no one else in his life. That she wasn't making a colossal mistake.

She glanced at his serious expression, one mixed with desire and concern. Kane might want her, but he was a gentleman in the ways he showed her his desire...except for that incident in the alley, where she'd been as willing a participant as he.

Her entire system shook in reaction. Foreplay, she thought. He'd readied her mind as well as her body. The heavy pulsing deep inside proved that, so did the anticipation of what awaited her.

She wanted to blame chemistry but she knew a lot more than that had pushed her to this moment. A lifetime of being treated as a sex object and not a person with feelings. Years of ignoring her own desires because she feared picking the wrong man, one who wanted her body but not the whole person. The final straw had come over the past month, when she'd taken on Charmed!—the vehicle to secure her sister's future and hold onto her aunt's past. While her sister dated, while Catherine registered and started culinary school, Kayla had deferred the rest of her education to run the business. She'd suppressed her own desires and needs. *What about what she wanted?*

She glanced at Kane. This man made her feel alive for the first time ever. Add what seemed to be a genuine caring and she couldn't go wrong. There might never be another man who valued *her*. Because there would never be another Kane McDermott.

She met his gaze. He was unattached and sexy, dynamic...and hers, for the night at least. The suspense and excitement built and she smiled. "Well, I guess that settles things."

"Does it?" He shoved his hands into the front pocket of his jeans. Tight jeans that molded against muscular thighs and showcased his obvious arousal.

She licked her dry lips. "Unless you've changed your mind."

"You were quiet for so long I was about to ask you the same thing."

Kayla drew a deep breath, as much for courage as for luck. Then she extended her hand.

A sexy grin edged the corners of his mouth and he intertwined his fingers in hers. "One stop first." He crossed to the front desk. He handed something to the clerk, whispering too low for her to catch what he said. "Ready?" he asked, turning back toward her.

Her stomach felt as if it hit the floor. "Ready," she murmured.

Everything that came next, the elevator ride and the walk down the dimly lit hall, all passed in a blur caused by near panic. Then she found herself alone with Kane in his hotel room. For a woman with limited experience, she wondered what had possessed her. She swung around, taking in the clutter. An open briefcase sat on the table, clothes lay scattered around and an unzipped suitcase had been shoved into the corner. The mess was so unfeminine, so like a man...so like Kane.

"You okay?" he asked.

"I'm fine."

"You're trembling."

She glanced at her surroundings once more. The king-size mattress in the center of the room drew her focus. What awaited her in that bed sent her imagination soaring. Kayla, Kane, hot bodies, tangled sheets... To her shock, her case of nerves calmed as she realized this was exactly where she wanted to be.

She looked at him. "I'm okay now."

"Kayla..."

"Yes?"

He cleared his throat. "Have you ever done this before?"

She raised her chin at the doubt in his tone. "Lots of times."

"Bull."

"Fine." She made for the door before his embarrassing, on-target questions humiliated her further. If her inexperience showed now, how disappointed would he be later?

She didn't get far. Two steps and he stopped her departure with a firm arm around her waist, drawing her close against his lean, hard body. His masculine scent pummeled her nerve endings, enticing her physically, assaulting her already raw senses. Her breasts tingled, her skin sizzled with fire and that wasn't the worst part. This man had the power to affect her emotions, too.

"Where are you going?" he asked.

"My mama always said if you can't do something right, don't bother doing it at all."

"Did I say you did anything wrong?"

She rolled her eyes and threw the blame squarely on him. "Not me, you."

"I did something wrong. What?"

"You questioned my experience. Not exactly the way to endear yourself to a woman, McDermott."

She forced herself to remain stiff and unyielding in his arms, even though she wanted to curl into him and feel his strength flow through her.

His heated breath fanned her neck. His cologne threatened to seduce her and make her forget common sense. She struggled against the seductive pull. "Let me go."

"Not until you answer the question I asked a minute ago and then I'll explain. If you don't like what you hear, I'll take you home myself. Have you done this before?" he asked again.

"A one-night stand in a stranger's hotel room? No. Happy now?"

"Not by a long shot. And that wasn't the question I was asking and you know it."

"Okay," she said, resigned. "Once in my senior year of high school and once more a few years ago." The first time she'd been young and inexperienced, scared but seduced into believing the guy had wanted her, not just a quickie in the back seat of his car. He'd gone to great lengths to convince her, and she'd bought his act. Then he'd gone bragging to his friends, and she'd never heard from him again. The second time had been years later. Another mistake, a futile effort to relieve the loneliness in her life.

She resented being forced to relive either time. "You want names and dates, too, Officer, or are the sketchy details enough?"

He jerked back, but kept his hand firmly around her waist.

"Well?" she asked when he remained silent. "Are

you going to keep grilling me like some cop or let me go home?"

"Neither."

His long exhale took her by surprise. Had he been as tense as she was about this encounter? Impossible. Men didn't get nervous.

Kayla straightened as best she could, trying to ignore that her behind now snuggled firmly against him. She didn't have to look back to know what male organ pressed hard and insistently against her. She gritted her teeth.

"Why is this so important?" she asked him.

"You said years." His hand brushed her hair off her face and he lay a warm, comforting cheek next to hers. "I want you so badly I can barely stand." His rough voice shook her body. The truth shook her soul. "If I didn't ask, if I didn't know, I'd have hurt you."

Her cheek remained cushioned next to his. He felt so right. Her stiff muscles relaxed, even as her body remained strung tight and begged for sexual release.

Kane loosened his hold, apparently assured she wouldn't run. She turned, crossing her arms in front of her and clutching her stomach in a death grip as she asked her next question. "And if you had...hurt me, I mean...you'd have cared?"

He swallowed so hard she saw his throat muscles at work. "Is that so hard to believe?"

"About a man, yes. About you, after this...no. I..." Her next words were interrupted by a knock on the door.

He held her gaze for a long second with a hot look that pulled his features taut and put sparks of need in his eyes. Need *she* inspired. The notion awed her.

"I've got it." He opened the door and waited as a man placed a room service cart with what looked like a thermos of coffee on the only free counterspace available in the room. "Fast work. I guess money does talk."

"What is that?" she asked.

"Payment." She raised one eyebrow in question. "For what's to come," he explained. Lifting the silver tray off the plate, he revealed two packages of instant hot cocoa mix.

"You remembered," she said, both pleased and impressed. This caring man had amazed her yet again.

"When an intelligent woman speaks, I listen. Besides how could I deny such a simple request? Especially when it will get me everything I want." His seductive smile caused her insides to twist into delicious knots only he could undo.

"Had for a cup of hot chocolate." She couldn't help but laugh. "I guess I'm easy," she murmured, rubbing her still-chilled hands against her jean-clad thighs for warmth. His gaze followed the movement, his eyes darkening with unmistakable sexual heat.

"Are you?" He walked to her slowly. His eyes never left hers as his hands went to the zipper on her jacket.

His knuckles grazed her chin as he made quick work of opening the zipper, his large hands brushing the sides open and off her shoulders. The jacket slid to the floor in a heap while his hands lingered. He gripped her upper arms hard, yet his fingers were shockingly gentle as they molded to her flesh beneath the constricting turtleneck.

His next maneuver surprised her. Strong hands slid through her hair, gliding and touching in a soft whisper of movement. Her headband joined the jacket on the floor, creating a pile of clothing destined to grow. Strong hands combed through her tangled hair. The tugging at her scalp felt erotically wicked. Without warning, a violent tremor took hold. Heat pounded between her thighs and a trickling liquid warmth followed in its wake.

Being with this man wouldn't be slow and easy. It wouldn't be controlled and simple to understand. She didn't want it to be. Her first step toward recognizing herself as a woman meant accepting what she'd believed impossible. A wild abandon existed in her soul, waiting for the opportunity to be set free.

Other men had touched—and they'd turned her ice-cold. No one else had inspired such gut-wrenching need. But Kane had seen beyond the packaging to the woman inside, and because he had, Kayla came together at last—body, heart and soul. She didn't care if she'd only known him one night, she felt so much more. She wanted him and she wouldn't, couldn't restrain the gnawing hunger any longer.

She recalled his last question. Was she easy? "For

you I guess I am," she murmured and stood on her tiptoes to place a full, openmouthed kiss on his lips.

His body shook and the tremors vibrated through her as he grabbed her waist and pulled her roughly against him. "Lady, do you have any idea what you do to me?"

Kayla gathered her courage and repeated his words of earlier that night. "No, but you could show me."

KANE EXPELLED A HARSH breath. In her playful innocence, she obviously had no idea she'd brought him too close, too fast. He hadn't held back tonight and looking into her clear gaze, he couldn't start now. He grabbed for her hand and placed it on the front placket of his jeans.

"Oh." Her gasp of surprise was telling.

If she were as smart as she was supposed to be, she'd pull back before things got out of hand. The rational part of him hoped she would. Instead she cupped him firmly in her palm and molded her fingers to the faded denim, tracing the weight of his arousal pushing restlessly against the restricting denim.

He closed his eyes and tried to think...of sports. Tonight's game, that ought to keep his mind off sex while her hand explored and his body contracted. Last thing he needed was to embarrass himself before things even got started. The weight and pressure of her fingers was driving him mad. And then she went to the button on his jeans. Baseball, he reminded himself. Bats, balls, stolen bases and home runs... Damn this was a bad idea.

He grabbed for her wrist. "Enough."

"Why?"

He met her startled gaze. "Ever hear of too much too soon?"

Understanding lit her embarrassed gaze while his traveled the length of her and back again. Large breasts rounded beneath the tight turtleneck top and rigid nipples pushed through the thin white material. Her jeans were fitted, accentuating full hips and generous curves. Kane had had his share of women, and they'd had one thing in common. They spent too much at the gym trying to be model-thin, or had put themselves on ridiculous diets he'd never understand.

Kayla had eaten what she pleased tonight and enjoyed every mouthful. And he'd enjoyed watching her. He wondered if her sexual appetite was as unbridled.

Twice and she hadn't been thrilled at the admission. What had those experiences been like for her? His groin still ached from a touch that hadn't been hesitant but...experimental. Despite the body made for sex and sin, this woman was fresh and new.

Too wholesome for someone like him. Yet he couldn't turn back. He needed her, something he wasn't ready to face now...and probably not ever.

"I don't really believe there's such a thing as too much, do you?" She touched a soft hand to his cheek and he knew. She trusted him, yet everything about *them* was a lie. He'd known enough about her going in to wrap her around his finger, and he'd done it easily. He hadn't counted on being floored himself. But he had been...as much as she.

Since she believed he'd be leaving the state after tonight, he could give them both a time to remember. No risk involved for either of them. She was too good at chipping away at the rough exterior he'd built and relied upon to survive. If not for the softness in her, if not for the softness she brought out in him, they'd be in a sweaty tangle on the floor by now. His throbbing body reminded him they hadn't gotten that far. Yet.

He held his hand toward her. "Why don't we find out?" Her fingers twisted in his, he led her to the oversize chair beside the table. He sat down and lowered her into his lap, facing him. "Still cold?"

She turned so she straddled his hips with her own and met his gaze head-on. "Not anymore." He heard a smoldering heat in her voice. "Or should I say yes so you'll warm me?"

Her impish grin was at odds with the questions in her eyes. Kane decided to erase those, as well as all rational thought once and for all. He wrapped his hands around her waist. "How about you say nothing at all?" he said and sealed his mouth to hers.

She tasted as good as before. She made him as hot as before—only faster this time. He pulled her shirt from the waistband of her jeans, needing to feel, taste and savor the sensations only she aroused. A willing partner, she helped, raising her arms to make his job easier, and before he could blink, he was facing his fantasy.

Ever since stealing a glimpse of Kayla Luck through a glass storefront window, Kane had been waiting for this. He just hadn't let it enter his conscious mind. It was there now. *She* was there now.

He traced the edge of white lace surrounding her plump breasts, feeling her soft flesh beneath his fingertips. Her chest rose and fell in time to her rapid breathing, but she held his gaze and didn't say a word.

"Don't take this the wrong way, but you're beautiful."

"Don't worry. If I let you get this far, I believe the compliment."

"Unlike this morning."

She shrugged. "I didn't know you this morning."

"And you do now."

She laughed and he discovered even her grin made him hard.

"I know what's important," she said playfully. "Isn't that what you said?"

He nodded and pushed the material beneath her breast, exposing all of her for view. The blood in his veins pumped fast and furious. "Still hot?" He placed a kiss on the distended tip of her nipple.

A strangled sound escaped her lips.

"I'll take that as a yes—which makes hot chocolate out of the question."

She stared at him wide-eyed.

"But I am hungry. How about you?" Reaching to

his side, he felt beneath the room service cart left by the hotel staff earlier and came up with a can of whipped cream. "Special request," he said.

"You think of everything, don't you?" she asked.

"I try." He shook the can with one hand.

She was already willing. He also wanted her hot...and wet...and enjoying every moment. She hadn't done much of that in the past and he wanted her to remember him even after he was gone. He didn't want her ever to forget.

With great show and care, he circled her nipple with a generous helping of whipped cream. Her smoldering gaze met his. "Something wrong?" he asked.

"It's cold." Laughter and anticipation lit her voice.

"Not for long." He lifted her breast in his hand, savoring the weight, the feel, the warmth and then he proceeded to devour his dessert until he was tasting beyond cold and sweet, until he was tasting Kayla.

Unfortunately for him, his plan worked too well. She lost herself in sensation. She moaned aloud, her thighs clenched and unclenched around his. And Kane knew she was past conscious thought, past the point of asking him to stop.

Which meant she trusted him. He glanced at her glazed eyes, and her honest face. A protest of his own rose to his lips. Before he could speak, her hips bucked against him and his coherency vanished. He met her thrusts with unrestrained pumping of his own until he thought he'd come right then. Lifting her up, he waited only for her to wrap her legs around his hips and he took the few steps needed.

Together they toppled onto the bed. In between spurts of laughter and the mess of the whipped cream, which she attempted to lick from his lips, they managed to stand and undress. Kane grabbed for his jeans and pulled a condom out of his wallet, realizing on some subconscious level, he'd been prepared for this. He'd made sure his wallet wasn't empty.

Shaking off the implications, he joined her on top of the mattress. She lay beneath him, naked and ready. *His*. He shook his head to clear that thought, but it remained. He pushed a strand of hair off her cheek, stuck there thanks to leftover whipped cream.

"I never realized making love could be fun," she said, out of breath.

He'd never laughed while having sex, either. At least he'd given her something after all. He grinned. "Sweetheart, you haven't seen anything yet." He shifted his weight and slipped his hand between her thighs.

She was everything he'd wanted her to be. Warm, slick and, if the sighs greeting his ears were any indication, she was definitely enjoying. He slipped one finger inside her moist heat.

"Kane?" His name came out on a groan.

"What?" Closing his eyes against the tension threatening to burst inside him, he eased his finger out...

"I'd rather you...I mean, we..."

He knew what she meant. But he wasn't ready. He wanted more for her than a fast tumble. More memories. He slipped his finger back in once more. "Patience is a virtue," he told her through clenched teeth.

"Then I'm not virtuous." As if to make her point, she wrapped her hand around his straining length and proceeded to pick up a rhythm that brought him to the brink.

"Point made."

Taking care of protection seemed more of a nuisance than it should. Then, grabbing her wayward hands, he yanked them above her head and held her wrists with one hand. With the other, he eased himself inside her, trying like hell to keep in mind it had been a long time for her.

Considering how perfect the fit, how intense the emotion she drew from him, this was a first for him as well. Kane held onto rational thought long enough to recognize he'd never felt like this before. Seconds before he climaxed in her arms, he knew he'd never feel like this again.

HE WOKE TO THE SOUND of rustling clothing. Kane rolled onto his back to see Kayla slipping back into her clothes. Last night came back to him in a rush of memory and sensation—because his body was rockhard. Despite that he'd slept with her twice, and that the sheets still carried their scent, he wanted her again. Wanted her more than he had the first time.

One glance and he knew she'd planned on slipping out before he awoke. Something he'd done himself and only now, being on the receiving end, did he realize how low a maneuver that actually was. The sense of loss shocked him.

She was leaving. Because she was sorry for what happened? Because she was embarrassed and couldn't face him? Or because, God help him, he'd been nothing more to her than a one-night stand? He couldn't stand the possibility, and in that fleeting second, he wanted more.

"Going somewhere?"

She glanced up from buttoning her jeans. Her hair fell around her face in easy waves, surrounding guilt-ridden, embarrassed eyes. "I was just..."

"Leaving?"

"Getting dressed. I would have woken you."

"Bull."

"You like that word."

"Only when it fits." He rose from the bed, ignoring that he was naked, and trying unsuccessfully to ignore her gaze following him across the room.

"I thought a clean break would be best. You're going back to New Hampshire later today anyway, so I figured, this way, no messy goodbyes." She turned a bright, sunny smile his way.

He shoved his hand into his pants pockets and fished through his wallet. What was he to her? She hadn't accepted his date until he'd pressured her into it with the lesson pretense. Was he a client she never wanted to see again or something more?

In his mind, the case had been closed long before

he slept with her. He knew she wasn't a prostitute, knew she had no knowledge of any ring that might exist. But she was the woman who'd slipped past his walls. No one had ever gotten that close before. If anything would kill the edge Reid was so worried about, the one that kept him alert and alive, this was it. A soft, caring woman.

Kayla Luck.

Kane drew a deep breath. It didn't matter why he'd come into her life. The fact remained that he had, and, in the process, he'd compromised himself, his principles, his case and his job. *Not bad for a night's work, McDermott.* He had to let her go. But the same part of him that wanted to kick himself for getting in too deep also needed to know. Could it all have been one-sided?

He turned toward her, wallet open. "We never agreed on a price, but I'm sure this will cover last night's...*lessons.*" She might not think she'd *taught* him anything. But she had. A very expensive and painful lesson. He tossed the wad of bills onto the bed.

Don't take the money. His heart seemed to hammer out the words in rapid beats. Furious with himself, he still needed to see her reaction, needed to know what he'd meant to her.

He looked over his shoulder. She'd paused in the process of pulling the baby-blue jacket onto her shoulders.

"What...is...that?"

"You said we'd see how things go." And they had. He thrust his hand toward the bed where the money sat, glaring and rude. "That's payment for services rendered."

4

KAYLA STARED AT THE MONEY on the bed in disbelief. "Payment." She forced the words from her dry throat.

"You said we'd see how things go."

Yes, she had...and now she knew. *Things* had been unbelievable, or so she'd thought. Special, sensual, incredible, fun, she couldn't come up with enough adjectives to describe how being with Kane had felt. Because he was leaving, she'd decided to slip out before he awoke. No goodbyes, nor forced smiles. No questions, like *will I see you again?* She'd been foolish enough to hope he'd look her up again on his own, no prompting.

She turned toward the bed. The money marred the mattress where she'd come close to falling hard. For a stranger. Her stomach cramped and she was reminded of another morning after. *It's been real, Kayla. Catch you around sometime.* Different man, another notch in some guy's bedpost. Kane had just been so much better at seducing her into denial before slapping her with reality. Men didn't want anything real with Kayla Luck. They never had, never would.

She squared her shoulders and forced a brave front. She refused to let him know how deeply he'd wounded her. "You're right, we never agreed on payment."

Unable to look into those dark eyes, she kept her gaze trained on a point behind him. "I said we'd see how things went...and..." The green bills caught her eye, mocking the instincts she'd trusted as well as her attempt at composure.

She paused, wanting to slam him, wanting to say last night hadn't been good enough to accept payment in return. But that wasn't her nature, though Catherine might have had a choice word or two for a man who'd crossed her, Kayla was different. She bent and grabbed her bag. Perhaps she no longer trusted her judgment in men, but she respected herself enough to be strong until she walked out that door. No man had the right to treat her like a prostitute.

Straightening, she met Kane's unreadable gaze. "Know what, McDermott? You and your payment can go to hell." She didn't know him well, but she'd learned enough last night to catch a flicker of emotion in his eyes now.

Relief mixed with regret? She shook her head, realizing she'd been searching for something to hold onto despite his crude offer. Apparently she harbored unhealthy illusions. For all his suave charm, Kane McDermott was no better than the rest.

Gathering her pride and her jacket, she ran for the door.

Kane didn't try to stop her.

"NO CASH EXCHANGED HANDS last night. Unless you can claim success, McDermott, I'd say case closed." Reid approached Kane from behind.

Kane eased back in his chair and forced himself to turn and look his superior in the eye. "She's clean, boss."

"Damn." Captain Reid crumpled a sheet of paper and slammed it into the trash. "Waste of manpower," the older man grumbled.

"Seems like," Kane agreed.

"Our informant could be blowing smoke, playing both sides for cash...but the teasers he gave us sounded legit. I really believed certain of our politicians were frequenting that place on the sly." The captain paced the short length of Kane's desk and back again before coming to a halt. "Any chance things happened before Ms. Luck's reign?"

Kane shook his head. "Doesn't seem possible. Not without her knowing. She was around during the aunt and uncle's days, she helped them out once in a while with classes and handled the books. Now she's running the place herself. If there was anything going on then or now, she'd know."

"Any chance she was tipped off, then turned those lovely charms your way? Any chance she got to you last night?"

"Conned me? None. The lady's innocent. I'd bet my badge."

"Really." The captain raised a knowing eyebrow before settling himself on the edge of the metal desk. "Now that's a first."

"What is? I always trust my instincts."

"But you never put that faith in another human being, especially a lady." He gave Kane a pointed look. "Until now." He stood and headed for his office.

Direct hit, Kane thought. He couldn't avoid the truth any longer. Couldn't avoid thinking, either, though that's what he'd tried to do since Kayla's abrupt departure this morning.

The captain was right. He *had* put faith in her and he'd let down his guard. For one ridiculous moment, he caught a glimpse of a life different than the solitary one he led. He'd been alone so long without a true connection to another person. But Kayla had shown him there was more than eating, sleeping and working. She'd made him feel alive and, foolishly, he'd wanted more. Not that he could have accepted, considering he was incapable of offering anything substantial in return.

Money in exchange for sex. That was one hell of an offer he'd made. He snorted in disgust. He'd set out to prove she wasn't a call girl, and had treated her no better than a hooker instead. The wounded look in her eyes hit him harder than when he'd been decked head-on with the butt of a gun. Guilt and regret twisted his insides.

A detective with years of experience questioning suspects, yet he botched the one chance he had with Kayla. In the end he'd done them both a favor. Interpersonal skills weren't his thing and now she knew it, too. Besides, the lady was too good at breaching his defenses, something he and his line of work couldn't afford. Letting her go hadn't been easy, but it had been necessary.

"McDermott."

Kane raised his gaze toward Reid's office. "Yeah, boss?"

The older man waved a sheath of papers in the air. "Report on my desk by tonight. Everything gels, case closed."

"Right."

"And you look like hell, so get the paperwork done and, remember what I told you, I don't want to see your sorry butt in here till the middle of next week."

Kane opted not to argue. His burning eyes told him he could use the sleep.

First things first. He shoved a sheet of white paper into the typewriter beside his desk. Paperwork would force him to relive last night in all but intimate detail.

He groaned. Those intimate details might not make it onto paper, but they were forever etched in his brain. He and Kayla had warmed each other up, and hot chocolate had nothing to do with the heat in the hotel room. Her full body meshed perfectly into his, her slick wetness made for an easy glide home.

Home? He slammed his fists onto the keys. What the hell was he thinking? The lady had been a one-night stand and he should be glad she'd walked out first; pleased he'd ended any soft thoughts she might

have entertained about her night with Kane Mc-
Dermott, New Hampshire salesman.

Ripping out the ruined sheet of paper, he crumpled it into his hands and tossed it into the trash. She
wasn't out of his life a few hours and he couldn't
concentrate.

This whole mess could have been avoided had he
listened to his gut. He'd seen too many fellow offi-
cers, fellow loners, fail with women. And Kane had
one additional strike against him. He didn't know
how to care about anything other than his job.

His father had bailed when Kane was five. His
mother died six years later when she walked in front
of a city bus with no thought to the son she left behind. Annie McDermott had a brother who disliked
kids as much as he liked booze, but an eleven-year-
old Kane had talked the old man into a deal. A place
to live enabling him to avoid foster care in exchange
for Kane's promise to raise himself and stay out of
the drunken man's way. His uncle upped the ante
and mooched his mother's death benefits from the
state. Kane considered it a small price to pay for independence.

He'd been on his own for longer than he could remember and he liked it that way. For some reason,
the words didn't bring the comfort they once had.

KAYLA DIDN'T WANT TO GO home and face a grilling
from her sister. After grabbing the first cab outside
the hotel, she'd stopped at a coffee shop near
Charmed! before deciding to immerse herself in

work. Anything to keep busy and not think. She still had boxes of her aunt's and uncle's personal things stored in the back and, though her sister had promised to help, today was as good a day as any to start rummaging through them. But she doubted even work would take her mind off Kane McDermott.

Every stretch and pull of her muscles as she walked reminded her of last night's activity. Her body still tingled in places he'd touched. If she blocked out this morning and focused only on the sensual pleasures he'd given, she became aroused once more. Apparently her body had become detached from her mind. Either that or she was losing it. The man had offered her money for sex. No matter how special *she* found the night, she'd been alone in her feelings.

The burgundy overhang of the brownstone storefront loomed ahead and she sprinted the rest of the way. She jammed the key into the lock, wondering if the sauna had cooled off. If Kane was as good at fixing equipment as he was at seducing women, it would have. She shook her head hard.

She had to admit he wasn't the only one at fault. She'd invested more hopes and dreams in Kane than a one-night stand deserved. He had been callous, yes, but he'd never promised her more than what they'd shared and that had been spectacular.

She took one step inside and knew the heat had stopped pumping high. No plumber necessary, which was about the only thing she could thank Mr. McDermott for.

Kayla made her way to the back room. Easing the door open, she groped for the light switch on the wall. She never found it.

Someone grabbed an arm and jerked her inside. The door behind her slammed shut, closing her in the pitch-black storage room. Before she could react, an arm grabbed her around the neck at the same time a hand clamped over her mouth. She tried to scream and tasted leather.

The more she struggled the tighter the grip became. Fear rose fast and furious inside her, but she listened to instinct and stilled.

"Smart lady. Now listen up." The gruff male voice sounded in her ear and she caught a whiff of his breath, a revolting mixture of stale liquor and cigarettes. "Where's the money?"

She shook her head from side to side. Catching her silent message, he eased the pressure of his hand off her mouth, but the bite of his fingers still stung. "I don't know..."

He jerked back on his arm, causing a shot of pain in her throat. "Wrong answer."

Kayla had no idea what he was talking about, but he obviously wouldn't believe her and she wanted out of there alive and in one piece. "Okay." The one word came out on a hoarse croak. She forced a painful swallow. "There's no money on the premises. I..."

"Kayla?" Catherine's voice sounded from the outside room. "Are you back there? The light's on out here and you can't hide forever. I want *details*."

Her assailant stiffened and muttered a harsh curse. He released his hold and shoved her hard. She stumbled headfirst into the concrete wall and, with the impact, dropped to the floor. Pain lanced through her skull just as the back door opened enough to show a sliver of light and allow her intruder to disappear, leaving her in darkness again.

"Kayla, I know you're in..." Catherine swung open the door and hit the switch on the wall, bathing the room in a harsh bright light. "Oh my God, what happened?"

Lifting her head was an effort, but Kayla managed. She took in the shambles of her once neat storage room and groaned. "He trashed the place."

"He who? What happened to you?" Her sister bent down beside her.

"I'm okay."

Catherine narrowed her eyes. "You don't look it."

"I'm fine." The steady pounding in her skull made those words a lie. Fighting the pain, she struggled to stand. A wave of nausea made it an impossible feat.

"Sit." Catherine eased her back down and propped her against the wall. "I'm calling the police."

Kayla nodded only to discover even that was a mistake. She closed her eyes. She didn't know what the intruder wanted, but he'd been convinced he would find it here.

Catherine returned and knelt down.

"What could he want, Cat?" Kayla's head swam and she couldn't think anymore.

"Don't try to talk. Here." Catherine placed a wet paper towel on Kayla's forehead.

The soggy rag dripped water down her face and Kayla laughed despite the pain and her tears. "You'll never challenge Florence Nightingale."

"Maybe not, but we've been tending each other's scrapes for years and I'm the best you've got." With a forced smile, Catherine balled up the sopping paper and tossed it onto the floor.

She grabbed Kayla's hand and eased herself beside her on the floor, huddling with her sister as they'd done many times as children. Kayla couldn't stop the uncontrollable urge to unburden herself to her sister—the only person she could trust. With her head on Catherine's shoulder, Kayla opened up about last night with Kane McDermott, talking until she was talked out.

And Catherine for once, remained silent, and Kayla was grateful.

"The police will be here in a few minutes," Catherine said at last. "And they'll take care of everything."

"I ALREADY TOLD YOU I walked in through the front door and he jumped me in the back." Raising her voice caused a set of drums to go off in Kayla's head. She placed Catherine's next attempt at first aid—a cold, wet but thankfully wrung out rag—against her scalp. She exhaled hard, fighting the nausea.

"The paramedics will be here any second." Kayla squinted at the young police officer as he spoke.

"Now back to what happened. He was looking for money and you *claim* there is none."

Catherine stepped forward into the man's direct line of vision. "Is this your first day on the job? Is that why you can't see *she's* the victim? Is this how they train you people today, to attack the helpless? Look, buddy, cop or no cop, I want your badge number and then I want your badge."

Kayla swallowed a groan at her sister's attitude, yet she couldn't understand the police treatment, either. Sirens began an insistent wail in the distance. At least she'd get an ice-pack rather than a barrage of questions she was too weak and nauseous to answer.

The officer eased back but not off. He lowered himself until he was at Kayla's eye level. "Look, the guy trashed the back room and did a number on you. Obviously he was looking for cash. Why? A little help from you will make things go easier."

"For whom?" Catherine jumped in. "She's not going to do your job for you and I want to know why you've been grilling her like she's a criminal instead of helping the victim."

"I'd like to know the answer to that, too."

"Kane." Kayla would recognize that voice anywhere.

He'd come back. A rush of powerful emotions hit her so fast her battered body and foggy mind couldn't decipher them now. She pushed herself to a standing position and turned as quickly as the pain in her head would allow.

"What the hell are you doing here?" Catherine asked.

Kayla winced at her sister's harsh tone. She never should have told Catherine even sketchy information about last night with Kane.

Kayla glanced at him. He stood in the entryway to the back room looking angry and dangerous, displaying the side she'd only glimpsed before. He ignored Catherine but when his gaze lit on hers, his expression softened.

He stepped toward her and held out his arms. She slid into his embrace. A comforting arm settled around her waist while the wall supported her back. "Well, Officer? Since when does the Boston P.D. grill injured victims?" he asked the junior cop.

The young officer flushed red. "I'm sorry, Detective, but..."

"Detective?"

Kayla's body went rigid and Kane winced. Not the way he'd wanted her to find out. He hadn't *planned* on her finding out at all. But nothing had gone as planned since he'd laid eyes on Kayla Luck.

He'd been halfway to the station house door when the 911 call had come in and the captain had waylaid him in the hall. Concern for Kayla had blocked out common sense, so here he was—with a job to do.

He took in her pale skin, glassy eyes and the red bruise on her forehead. He'd botched this "case" but no more. He took her arm despite her token resistance.

"Where are you taking her?"

Kane glanced at the blonde he'd met briefly last night, the one with flashing green eyes who'd just given the junior officer a tongue-lashing. "To the nearest chair. What are you, her sister or her guard dog?"

She opened her mouth but Kayla interrupted first. "Catherine, don't. He's right. If I don't sit I'll be sick."

He muttered a curse, then led her into the outer room.

With her leaning against him for support, Kane was reminded of last night. His body reacted with instant and urgent need. Ignoring her wasn't an option, acknowledging and distancing himself was.

Kayla accepted his help only until she reached the chair, then jerked out of his grasp and collapsed into the high-backed cushioned seat.

He knelt beside her. "Kayla…"

"What is it, *Detective?*" She spat the word like a curse. Her eyes remained closed, an effective physical barrier. He'd obviously added to the damage he'd already done. Her emotional walls were in place—just like his.

The paramedics came barging through the door, saving him from having to answer. As they examined her, he had time to reflect. He didn't like what he concluded.

He'd put his emotions before his case. Worse, he put this woman at risk. He glanced at Kayla. Bad enough he'd slept with her, but believing for an instant he could have more than one night had been insanity. Foolishness that could only lead to destruction. He'd broken his cardinal rule: he'd gotten involved.

If he'd maintained a distance, he would have been thinking more clearly. He would never have let her walk out the door this morning. Kayla's ignorance about illegal activities at Charmed! didn't mean those activities didn't exist. The captain was right. Kayla had gotten to him and in the process he'd compromised not only the case but her safety.

"Okay." The paramedic in the blue jacket stood. "Looks like a concussion and some bruising in the neck area."

A quick glance told him Kayla was still leaning back with her eyes closed in the large office chair. Red fingerprints marred the white skin on her throat and Kane's gut clenched in anger so strong it blinded him. No one had the right to touch her. Forcing his mind to clear, he let his gaze travel downward. She hadn't changed out of last night's clothes. She hadn't yet been home.

Behind her, Kane saw Captain Reid enter the storefront. Kane turned to the paramedic first. "Hospitalization?" he asked.

"She refused, which is fine as long as someone's around to watch over her and bring her in if necessary."

"Someone is," the sister chimed in.

For the moment, Kane ignored her. "Restrictions?" he asked the younger man.

"Complete bed rest, wake her every two hours,

check coherence, understanding, pupil dilation... you know the drill."

"Got it."

"No problem," the sister said, eyeing Kane with a scowl.

With the paramedic gone and the captain getting briefed by the officer who'd arrived first on the scene, Kane turned his focus on Catherine. "You're Catherine, right?"

"And you're the louse who used my sister."

He didn't see any point in mentioning the *using* had been mutual. Kayla had been dressed and ready to walk out on him first. "You don't know anything about it."

"I know enough and I doubt that official-looking guy in the suit would appreciate that you slept with a...what was Kayla, anyway? A suspect?"

"What makes you think that?"

"The way junior was grilling her." She jerked her thumb toward the uniformed officer.

"Leave it alone, Catherine."

"Because you say so?"

"Because I promise you she won't get hurt again." He'd make sure of that.

She narrowed green eyes that reminded him of her sister's. "Prove yourself and we'll see."

He didn't need the aggravation of an overprotective sister at this stage in the investigation, which was by no means over. And yet he couldn't help admire the fierce protectiveness and a pang of regret lanced through him. He'd never had anyone to look out for him. "Go check on Kayla," he muttered.

"I'll be watching you, McDermott, if that's even your real name." Catherine returned to her sister's side and Kane made his way over to Reid.

"Looks like things are heating up," Kane said.

"It looks like a botched robbery," the captain countered. "She walked in too soon."

Kane shook his head, his instincts screaming in protest.

"Nothing taken, nothing missing," the junior officer said. He glanced at his notepad. "But the lady claims the assailant was looking for cash she doesn't have."

"The night's take?" Reid asked.

The officer shrugged. "I hadn't gotten that far in my questioning."

Kane pinned him with an accusing glare. "Because you need to work on your technique. Grilling victims like suspects isn't doing your job."

Reid glanced back and forth between the two men, settling his gaze on the uniformed cop. "Get back to work. We'll talk later." The younger man took the hint and headed for the room that had been ransacked. "Could be coincidence," Reid said.

Kane shook his head.

"She help you any?" He pointed to Kayla.

"She still doesn't know what last night was about." And he wasn't looking forward to enlightening her.

"You're certain she wasn't tipped off about us and canceled activities last night?"

"Convince yourself. Have a talk with the lady."

Reid nodded and walked over to Kayla and her sister. Kane made himself scarce and strolled the perimeter of the small outer room instead. By the time the captain returned, Kane realized Kayla had turned this place into a reflection of herself. Books lined the metal shelving on the back wall, the topics wide and varied.

"You're right."

Shoving his hands into his pockets, he turned to his superior. "She's as much in the dark as we are," Kane said.

"Seems that way. She's bright and can hold her own in conversation but if she's lying about her knowledge, I'd eat my badge, like you said. None of the signs were there. As for the sister, I wouldn't want to fall into that mouth again, but I doubt she knows anything, either."

"Kayla's in danger." The knowledge sent a flood of emotion shooting through his veins. He welcomed the rush of adrenaline but not the depth of caring she drew from inside him. But he meant to keep his promise to Catherine. He meant to keep her safe.

"That's debatable. I'm not convinced this was anything more than a bungled job. A druggie wanting cash, hoping for a quick getaway, and coming up empty, maybe."

Kane shook his head. "Put someone on her."

"Can't spare more manpower on a hunch, Mc-

Dermott, not even yours. The most I can give you is surveillance, an hourly drive-by."

Kane shoved his hands into his jean pockets. "Not good enough."

"It'll have to be."

"For you maybe. But I'm taking that R&R you seem to think I need."

Reid raised an eyebrow. "To do what?"

"Baby-sit her myself if I have to. Instinct has kept me alive and I won't ignore it now."

"You too personally involved with this one?"

The words hit the intended target, but Kane refused to back down. "No."

"Whatever you say. You've got one week, but this is strictly off-duty. What about the sister?"

"I don't need two targets and, considering she's not involved in running the business, she's not in any immediate danger."

"I agree."

"So I want her out of the picture."

Reid glanced over at the two sisters with their heads bent close together and his chuckle filled the small room. "Good luck," he said and laughed again.

Kane didn't know whether the older man referred to Kane's ability to lose Catherine or his self-imposed week alone with Kayla. Either way he needed all the luck he could get.

5

THE ICE HAD BEGUN TO HELP her head. Even the nausea was no longer as bad. And then Kane spoke. "I'm taking you home."

His deep voice—still sexy to her ears—penetrated the remaining fuzziness in her brain. Kayla's stomach revolted at the thought. "I think I'm going to be sick."

Catherine grabbed for the nearest garbage pail, gaining a smile from Kayla despite how lousy she felt. "I don't think that's necessary." She turned on Kane. "I'm not going anywhere with you." Although her talk with Captain Reid had been enlightening, she still didn't know enough.

Apparently Kane's superior knew nothing about Kane and Kayla's late-night activities. Unlike other men, he hadn't been quick to brag that he'd scored with Kayla Luck. She wondered what that meant other than the fact that he didn't want to jeopardize his career.

The captain had questioned her about her business and clientele but was less than forthcoming about the reasons behind the police interest. He said he'd leave the divulging to his best detective. She suppressed a cynical laugh. Kane was good all right, at more things than just his job.

He crouched down until they were eye level. Razor stubble covered his cheeks, adding to the dangerous edge she'd only imagined before. The musky scent of his skin mixed with subtle aftershave heightened her awareness and put her senses into overdrive.

He bore no resemblance to the salesman who'd wined and dined her the day before, yet he was still the same man who intrigued her on a primal level. A man she didn't know. Yesterday's clean-cut appearance had obviously been another lie for her benefit. She had the distinct impression she now faced the real Kane McDermott.

She cradled her head in her hands and glared at him.

"You might not like me much right now. Hell, I'm not too thrilled with myself. But you aren't going home alone. It isn't safe."

"I agree," Catherine said. She folded her arms over her chest and waited.

"Would you please find something to do?" Kane muttered. "I'll talk to you later."

Catherine glanced at her sister. Kayla didn't like it, but she and Kane had unfinished business. "It's okay." With a nod, her sister headed for the back room.

"She always act like your mother?" he asked.

"Only when I'm being threatened."

"And that's what you think I'm doing?"

"I don't know that any more than I know who you really are. Last night was obviously a setup." She ignored the hurt the knowledge brought. "You're investigating me and my business. What for?"

His deep inhale warned her she wouldn't like what came next. "Prostitution."

Her hand moved of its own volition, cracking across his roughened cheek. Tears quickly followed. She swiped at them with her sleeve but he'd seen anyway. He didn't flinch, but in his eyes she viewed the same glimmer of emotion she'd caught last night. He masked it just as fast.

He was good at hiding his feelings and even better at hiding himself.

She swallowed over the painful lump in her throat that threatened to grow larger. Not only had he treated her like a hooker, but he'd *thought* she was one, too. "I didn't know detectives were into such *hands-on* investigation."

"Last night had nothing to do with the investigation."

Kayla folded her arms across her chest and remained silent. Her mama had another expression she'd ingrained into her girls: Give a man enough rope and he'd hang himself with it.

"The date, the setup, the dinner...those were part of the job," he admitted. "What came after wasn't." The subtle darkening of his eyes spoke of sexual heat and need. The softening of his features hinted at something more. "By the time we finished dinner, I knew you were innocent," he said.

Kayla inhaled. Mama was wrong in this case. Kane wasn't hanging himself. He'd taken a step toward redemption, not further condemnation. Yet how could she believe his words when everything that came before had been based on a lie?

She'd given her body to him in ways that bespoke of trust. She could have given her heart. He'd repaid her faith with the deepest violation she could imagine. But she still sensed an innate decency. One she wanted to believe in.

"Do you always offer money to the women you sleep with?" she asked.

Silence greeted her. Apparently she trod on sacred ground. "How reassuring," she said dryly. "My sister will take me home."

"Not unless you want her in the line of fire."

"There's no danger." Kayla swept her hand in the air, gesturing to the expanse of the room. Her head pounded in time to the motion. She winced but continued. "Look around you. No valuables, no merchandise...nothing. The guy didn't find what he was looking for. He won't be back." Despite the pounding pain, she put all her energy into convincing him so he and his lies would disappear.

He shrugged. "Depends. Is that why you don't have an alarm system here? There's nothing anyone would want?"

She nodded, then regretted the jerky motion. She gripped the armrests of the chair until the dizziness and pounding subsided.

He placed a firm hand on her thigh. He might

have meant to steady her, but his touch did more than reassure, it aroused—aroused buried feelings as well as sexual need.

"Do you have a burglar alarm at home?" he asked.

She cleared her throat. It still hurt to speak. "Don't need one. The guy probably thought he'd get money, then he was interrupted. He won't bother me again."

"I disagree and if I'm right and your sister gets hurt, will you be able to live with yourself?"

He'd hit her weakness and obviously knew it. Kayla wouldn't risk Catherine's life just to get Kane McDermott out of hers. "You're slime, you know that, Detective? You want to act as my personal home safety system? Fine. Park your car in the driveway and have a blast. Just remember to turn on the heater. I don't want your death on my conscience."

"Careful, Kayla," he said in that husky voice that caused an erotic tingling deep inside. "I might begin to think you care."

"Fat chance."

"Same with me hanging out in my car. The paramedics said you vetoed the hospital so you need someone to watch over you."

She narrowed her eyes. "And you're offering your services?" The thought of spending any time with this man who pulled her mind, her heart and her body in opposing directions was impossible.

She didn't trust her response to him, yet she trusted him to keep her safe. The contradiction wasn't lost on her. It was just one of many. "No way are you staying with me."

"You won't put your sister at risk, which leaves you alone. What if the guy shows up again? You were no match for him the first time. What makes you think you'll do a better job injured?"

"Like I said, you're slime, McDermott."

"I never argued the point, Ms. Luck."

Kayla saw Captain Reid approach. "I'm through here. Feeling better?" he asked.

"If I don't move," she said wryly.

He turned to Kane. "Remember what I said. Call if things turn serious—and enjoy your time off." The older man walked out into the cold afternoon.

"Time off?"

"Looking after you," Kane said. "And before you argue, remember I already won this argument. I'll go square things with Catherine."

She opened her mouth and shut it again. He might have played on every weakness she possessed at the moment, but he was right. Catherine wouldn't leave her for the night unless she knew she had protection. Kayla wouldn't be comfortable alone in the first floor of the old two-family house in which they lived. She loved the many windows because they let in light, but they left her vulnerable. Besides, she could barely lift her head.

Like it or not, she needed Kane.

"THIS PLACE IS A BURGLER'S dream," Kane muttered to himself. He paced the kitchen and small family area of the rented house. One step inside the unprotected home had cemented his decision to stay no matter how high the personal risk.

He'd waited outside the bedroom while Kayla changed into a T-shirt he'd found in a drawer filled with satin and lace, scented with the tempting fragrance his body associated with Kayla Luck. Her full breasts and soft flesh were known to him now. Desire and arousal would be his companions as long as he remained in this house.

Apparently so would longing and misplaced dreams. He'd settled her into bed, a pastel, feminine mass of ruffles and pillows. A safe haven that like Kayla reminded him of warmth, home and a sharing of lives. Things he never had and never would.

She was a luxury he couldn't afford. They hadn't just shared quick and easy sex, the kind that left both parties unfulfilled after the initial peak subsided. With Kayla it was complicated, involved and made him inefficient in his job, the one area of life he'd always been able to count on before.

He scrounged through the old wooden kitchen cabinets and found a can of soup. She needed something to eat and this was about all he was capable of making without turning her stomach even more. He'd check her again and then fix her a warm meal.

He entered her room and watched her in silence. Eyes closed, pale skin and blond hair falling over her cheek. She looked like an angel. His angel, he thought and stifled a curse. More softness he didn't need. *Focus on the job, McDermott.* He eased himself to sit beside her on the bed. The mattress shifted under his weight. She rolled toward him and moaned.

The sound twisted his gut. "Are you in pain?"

"Is that a rhetorical question?" Her eyes remained tightly closed, her arms wrapping the down comforter even more tightly around her body.

"I can't give you anything except Tylenol."

"I...took...some." Her teeth began to chatter. "Can you turn up the heat?"

"I already did." He'd anticipated the chills. Once the aftermath of her ordeal hit and her adrenaline levels decreased, he'd expected some reaction.

"Not...working."

"How about a cup of hot soup?"

"Can't sit up."

Kane muttered a prayer for strength and slid beneath the covers. She curled into his waiting warmth. Her soft curves molded against him and her satisfied sigh echoed in his ears. Two things hit at once. A hot, urgent desire to be inside her, and the need to protect her from further harm.

Reminding himself she needed his body heat and not *him*, he wrapped his arms around her and buried his face in her hair, the only advantage he'd take under the circumstances. "Better?" he asked.

"Much."

Silence settled around them, seeming to bounce off the walls of her room. A sense of contentment followed. Kane fought against it.

Without trying, she wove a spell he didn't understand, made him desire things he couldn't have. He inhaled her fragrant scent and felt himself being pulled deeper.

"I need you." She spoke so softly he had to strain to hear.

"I'm here now." The only promise he was willing to make.

BRIGHT SUNLIGHT SHONE through the bedroom window. Kane groaned and squinted into the glare. "Worse than a damn hangover," he muttered, rolling over and burying his face in his pillow.

As a cop used to undercover work, waking Kayla every two hours hadn't left him irritable and beat. Lying beside her, holding her and listening to her soft moans each time she moved did him in. The last check had been—he looked at his watch—an hour ago. She'd been light-headed but okay.

"Kayla?" He glanced over to find an empty bed and sat up fast. Throwing off the covers, he walked to the hallway bathroom. The sound of running water greeted him and he rolled his eyes at her foolishness. What made her think she could handle a shower alone?

He tried the doorknob and it turned. At least she hadn't locked herself inside. He opened it a sliver. "You okay in there?"

"Not really." Her voice sounded weak.

Kane didn't wait for permission. He barged inside. The bathroom was compact and steam floated around him. The scent of lemons hovered in the air. He ripped aside the shower curtain to find Kayla sitting on the floor of the porcelain tub, her head between her legs.

He slammed his fist against the large faucet and shut the water that had been pelting her body. "Can you lift your head?"

"Not by myself," she said, the words muffled.

"What the hell did you think you were doing?" He stepped barefoot into the wet tub, braced his hands beneath her arms and pulled her into a standing position.

"Taking a shower."

"I noticed." Droplets of water clung to her bare skin. He had a sudden desire to lick them off one by one. Instead he pushed her wet hair off her forehead so he could look into her eyes. He never got the chance.

She collapsed, unable to stand on her own. He swore and swung her into his arms, grabbing a towel before making his way back to the bedroom. Her wet skin soaked through the T-shirt and jeans he'd kept on the night before—more as a physical barrier to temptation than for modesty's sake. But barriers meant little when he had Kayla naked and needy in his arms. She clung to him, her head nestled on his shoulder and her wet body snug against him for warmth.

She trusted him. Impossible, he thought. He'd given her no reason. She needed someone and he was available. "You should get dressed." He placed her on the bed and wrapped a towel around her shaking shoulders.

"I just wanted a shower, but..." Her teeth began to chatter.

"Too much too soon. Especially on an empty stomach." He rummaged through her drawers again and pushed the most flimsy things aside. She'd need help, and he'd be wrapping a bra around her full breasts. His hands would be too close, his mouth too tempted. He settled on plain white, no frills, things that covered as much as possible. Then he picked a shirt, a man's football jersey. He didn't dwell on where she got it. At least it was large enough to keep him from staring. He was in too deep already.

"Here." He walked back to the bed. She still sat huddled in a tight ball. He worked the shirt over her head. "Raise your arms." She complied and her breasts lifted higher, her darkened nipples inches from his face.

"To serve and protect," he muttered as a reminder.

"What?"

"Nothing."

"Then stop mumbling. This is embarrassing enough already." He ditched the bra. Better to get this over with.

She wiggled a bit and the shirt fell around her generous hips.

"Think you can handle these?" He dangled a pair of briefs from his fingertips.

"Yes." She blushed scarlet. At least her coloring looked better than before. He turned to give her some privacy. A couple of deep breaths and he had himself under control.

"Thank you, Kane."

He turned. "No problem."

She lay propped back against the pillows. Soft hair fell around her face. A yearning gripped his insides hard.

"The steam made me weak," she said.

"You don't get out of that bed without my permission." Finding her on the tub floor had taken years off his life.

A weary frown crossed her lips. "I need sleep."

"First, you need to eat."

"Looking out for me, catching me when I fall, cooking my meals... Careful, McDermott, or I might think you care for more than your case."

He caught the teasing in her voice. "Fat chance."

She met his gaze. "Same with me following orders. I'm not some flunky you can boss around."

The words were stronger than her voice, but he accepted her warning. Once she felt better, Kane would have his hands full keeping her in line and out of harm's way. "What are you, Ms. Luck?"

"Your equal and I suggest you remember that."

His respect for her rose once more. She'd taken a beating, but she kept pulling herself up. Kayla was a fighter. He liked that about her. She could handle herself, but this wasn't an ordinary situation. When she felt stronger, he'd question her about her aunt and uncle's dealings.

Meanwhile, he wasn't about to lighten the severity

of her situation. "You take care of yourself or I'll cuff you to the bed." He gestured to the wrought-iron headboard behind her pillows.

She grinned. "First whipped cream, now bondage. Are you kinky, Detective?"

"Keep that up and you'll find out." The sudden banter and teasing caught him by surprise. So did the vision of her naked, shackled to the bed, eager to play sexual give-and-take.

Her eyes darkened. He wondered if she was considering the possibilities, then reminded himself he'd had his one night. He refused to take another.

Kane rose. Her fingers around his wrist stopped his escape. Warmth seeped into the places she touched.

"Running away?" she asked.

"Getting you food." Before he drew her down onto the mattress and gave in to baser, misplaced desires. Before he let himself drown in all she had to give.

She released her grip and struggled to a sitting position. "Okay."

He raised a suspicious eyebrow.

"What's wrong?" she asked.

"You gave in."

"Don't sound so surprised. I know what's good for me." She grinned. "Besides, we already established I'm easy."

KANE DISAPPEARED into the hall. Kayla leaned back against the pillows and groaned. Sparring with him had sapped what little strength she had left. The dizziness was better, but Kane was right—she needed to eat. Food would give her the energy to get out of this bed, deal with her aunt and uncle's legacy, and confront Kane, all on her terms.

Kane. What did he want from her? And what did she want from the tough cop?

"Lunch." He saved her from having to answer.

Standing in the doorway, he was the epitome of every fantasy she'd never allowed herself to have. A strong, capable, caring, sexy man...concerned about her.

She glanced at the mug in his hands, pushing herself to a sitting position. "Vegetable?"

"Was there another kind?" he asked wryly. He handed her the white ceramic cup. The steaming mug warmed her hands. She inhaled and the aroma of beef stock and vegetables drifted upward. Her stomach grumbled aloud. He chuckled.

Refusing to be embarrassed, she took a grateful sip before meeting his amused gaze. "Canned soup at its finest."

Laugh lines formed in attractive crinkles around his eyes. "It's the closest thing to homemade you'll get from me. Come on. Drink up."

She narrowed her gaze. "Do you take such good care of all your assignments, Detective?"

His hand went to her cheek. She felt his touch shoot straight to her heart. "Don't sell yourself short, Ms. Luck."

The jangling of the phone jarred them. She darted

a glance at the phone. "Catherine thinks she needs to protect me from you."

"I already reassured her earlier, but apparently she needs proof. Besides, she's right." His dark gaze met hers, his barely readable expression revealing hidden knowledge and a deep yearning need. Her stomach twisted again but hunger wasn't the cause.

The phone rang once more, breaking the connection. "Better let Catherine know you're okay or she'll be showing up on your doorstep." He grabbed the cup and placed it on the nightstand before walking toward the door.

She picked up the phone. "I'm fine," she said without preamble.

"You won't be if I don't get my take and I want the books."

She gripped the receiver hard. "Who is this?"

"Have you forgotten already?"

The gravelly tone chilled her. "You attacked me."

Kane whirled around and stalked back to the bed. A strong, supporting hand cupped her shoulder. When she glanced up, he merely nodded, urging her to keep talking.

"That was just a preview," the voice on the phone said.

She drew courage from Kane's presence. "What do you want?"

"For you to stop playing dumb. My share and a resumption of activities."

"I don't..."

"You can't cut my man out, and you can't run this

on your own. Get the money. I'll be in touch." A click and she was disconnected.

He grabbed the phone out of her hand and punched in a succession of numbers, then muttered a curse.

"What?" she asked.

"Untraceable. Probably a damn phone booth." He placed the phone back in the cradle, then turned to Kayla. "What did he say?"

She couldn't meet his gaze. "Seems you were right. Charmed! is a front for something illegal, after all."

The anger she'd held toward him left in a rush. Fear still pulsed inside her, but she needed answers and knew just where to find them.

Kayla threw off the sheets. Her head pounded in opposition to the sudden movement, but she forced herself to swing her legs over the side of the bed.

"Hang on." His hand on her bare thigh stopped her. Blazing heat seared her to the core.

He didn't speak. Neither did she. Sexual tension crackled in the air between them, fierce and alive. His large hand remained on her bare skin.

"Where are you going?" His roughened voice didn't surprise her. She'd be shocked if she could speak herself.

"I—" She stopped and cleared her throat. "To the office. There are boxes, things of my aunt's I haven't looked through yet." Not that she believed for a minute that her mother's sister would be involved in anything as sleazy as prostitution. But the fact remained there was obviously much she didn't know about her newly inherited business.

"I'll have them brought by along with a change of clothes for myself. We can go through them together."

Together. The word caused an involuntary shiver. She liked the sound. Too much. But once again he was right. After her pathetic shower attempt, a trip to the office seemed ridiculous.

"Thank you." She hated ceding control to Kane but she had no choice for now.

She focused again on his large hand still covering her thigh. His thumb moved back and forth, his finger gliding over her skin. What was meant as comfort her body read as sensual. The rhythmic motion of his hand released a steady beat between her thighs.

His touch ruled her senses, but she still had presence of mind. He had set her up and used her in the name of his job. For him, it was a professional relationship after all.

She glanced at his taut jaw and his darkened gaze. Or was it more than professional? Her heart kicked into faster speed as the past twenty-four hours came back to her in a rush. The minute he'd slept with her, he'd compromised his job. He'd taken time off to care for her when his boss vetoed protection. He'd talked her sister into spending time with a friend. And he'd crawled into her bed to keep her warm. In Kayla's book that went beyond police protection.

The answers about Charmed! might have to wait,

but the ones about Kane would not. "You could have left. Even your boss wouldn't authorize this kind of protection."

His hand stilled and his eyes cleared. "My gut told me the case wasn't over yet."

She swallowed hard and forced herself to continue. She might never get another chance to find out the truth. "And that's the only reason you're here?"

"If I'd trusted my gut instinct I wouldn't have left you alone. You wouldn't have been attacked."

"Guilt."

"Reality."

"Whatever." Let him think what he chose. Neither answer accounted for the more intimate aspects of their relationship...like the hard arousal pressed against her belly each time she'd awakened in his arms last night.

"So you're making up for...what?" she asked.

"Sleeping with you made me lose my focus." His grip on her leg loosened and he stood. "It won't happen again."

"I see," she murmured. A mixture of understanding and awe filtered through her. *She'd gotten to him.* She'd penetrated the tough exterior and made Kane McDermott feel. She didn't know what women had come before her, but she doubted with all the strength borne of feminine instinct that he'd ever lost focus because of a night of hot sex.

And hot sex with Kane wasn't enough. The realization came to her as clear and strong as the sunlight suddenly streaming through the window. She blinked against the harsh glare. He walked across the room and drew the shades.

Kayla folded her arms over her chest and lay back against the pillows. She'd gotten to him once. She could do it again. She had as much to prove to Kane as to herself. Her ability to trust her instincts was at stake. She'd read him so wrong that first night. She had to know she was right about him now.

Exhaustion threatened, but she couldn't give in. She intended to test his resolve. He might think he was here as her protector to atone for his sins. Was he in for a surprise.

She glanced across the room. He stood, legs braced apart, staring out the slit in the blinds. She knew the muscles in those legs, the feel of him pulsing in her hand. She knew how it felt to be comforted and held through the night.

She wanted more from Detective Kane McDermott than his guilt-induced protection. She wanted the chance to see if they had a chance. To see if this man was the one to breach her own walls, and show her men—and relationships—had potential. To do that she had to get past his barriers.

And Kayla intended to get what she wanted.

6

KAYLA SUSPECTED HE'D FIGHT her by erecting barriers so high, she'd have to learn to mountain climb to achieve her goal.

"Kane?" He turned at the sound of his name, his hands tucked in his front jean pockets.

"Thank you."

"For?"

"If you'd come over here, I'd tell you." She couldn't trust herself to stand and she couldn't talk to him if he stood so far away. She had more than physical barriers to breach. She just hadn't yet learned what the others were.

He walked over and lowered himself onto the bed, causing the mattress to dip beneath his weight. Kayla drew her legs up and scooted closer to the edge. Closer to him.

She placed a hand on his arm. Muscles tightened beneath her fingertips. She didn't loosen her grip. "I appreciate your being here."

"Why? I lied to you from the second we met."

She'd expected to have to force truths out of him. Instead he'd given her the opening she sought. "Because you were doing your job. I realize that now."

"If I was doing my job, you'd have been protected before you got hurt."

She laughed, but knew better than to shake her head. Eating had helped, but she still felt drumbeats when she moved too fast. "Sometimes we mistake what our jobs are. I remember one night when I was younger. Catherine wanted to go out with her friends. I knew these friends were trouble, that she was headed in the wrong direction. So I snuck into her room and stole her wallet and what little money she had inside. She went anyway, and got caught sneaking out of a restaurant without paying the hefty bill." Kayla gnawed the inside of her cheek, remembering the night the police officer had brought her sister home.

His strong hand touched her cheek. "What's your point?" he asked in a gruff voice.

"We raised each other. It was my job to look out for her and I blew it."

"Was she arrested?"

"No. The owner refused to press charges. He gave her a job washing dishes instead. The point is, I didn't do my job, but looking back, it wasn't mine to do. Just like the minute I walked out of that hotel room, I wasn't yours to look out for anymore."

"I agree with you about Catherine. As for me, I was still on a case."

She raised an eyebrow. "Sleeping with me was work-related?"

"Don't twist my words."

"Then let the guilt go." Kayla couldn't reach him if

he hid behind his job and sense of duty. "Look, when you were a teenager, did you ever get in an argument with your mother, then storm out into the street?"

He met her question with a vacant stare.

Curious she pushed on. "At that point, there wasn't anything she could do to stop you from getting into trouble."

"There wasn't a damn thing she could have done about anything. She was dead."

Her mouth opened and closed again just as fast. "I'm sorry."

"Don't waste your time feeling sorry for her. She killed herself. Took herself out of the game."

Leaving her child behind. Kayla knew better than to voice pity for the boy he'd been. She was grateful enough for the revelations. She wasn't about to discourage them by suffocating him in emotion. "And your father?" she asked.

"Took a hike when I was five. Is there a point to all this?"

A smile tipped the edges of her mouth. "There was, but you've cut off every one I was about to make."

Kane let the tension ease out of his shoulders. She didn't treat him with the sad look or pitying expression his friends, teachers and the authorities had used in his youth. He hadn't voiced his story again until now, but wasn't surprised he'd confided in Kayla.

He'd known many women. None affected him on

any level other than physical. None attempted to challenge him. He'd met his match with Kayla and he respected her for it. Respected her far more than women who played the weak heroine to get his attention and into his bed.

He'd begun having sex early in his teens, too often he'd come to realize. Later he'd become smarter, more discriminating. Only one thing remained constant. He came and went with no thought to looking back or revealing inner truths. Not so with Kayla. After all she'd been through—thanks to him—she deserved a little honesty.

But that wasn't the sole reason for his confidences now. He didn't want to think about why he wanted to share the most painful parts of his life with this woman.

She shifted, the movement revealing pale skin and an expanse of thigh that aroused him in an instant.

"My point is you aren't responsible for me," she said, meeting his gaze.

Primitive possession flooded his system. "The hell I'm not."

In the face of his roar, she didn't blink.

He admired her spunk. "You're my responsibility at least until this case is over, so let's drop that part of the conversation now."

"Okay."

He hadn't expected her to give in without an argument. "So you aren't angry?"

"Not about the initial investigation."

"And what came after?"

"Pheromones," she explained.

"What?"

"Two people attracted to each other by stimuli they can't control." He'd forgotten the intellectual side of this beautiful woman. "A chemical reaction," she went on. "So if you're still blaming yourself for losing focus, don't. I'm equally at fault."

"Meaning?"

"I wanted you, too." She fiddled with the hem on her jersey without meeting his gaze. This was the Kayla he'd first met. The innocent that threatened to chip away at his heart, if he let her.

Which he wouldn't. But he couldn't let her last statement go unchallenged. He had to know. "'Wanted' as in past tense?" he asked.

She shrugged and leaned back into the pillows. "Why ask? You're a man of your word. You said it won't happen again. Does what I want really matter?"

He could drown in emotion, in her. "Everything you want matters."

Her expression grew still, then a tear spilled from the corner of one eye. "No one's ever said that to me. I'm thankful for you, Kane."

A low growl escaped from his throat. "I don't want your gratitude."

"Then what *do* you want?"

"That's a loaded question."

"I know. That's why I asked." An impish smile played around her mouth, even as she wiped away a tear.

Kane knew what he wanted. Kayla, soft and giving beneath him. But she was right. He'd laid down the law. *It wouldn't happen again.* But he knew what Kayla needed—to be reassured that *she* counted. It was the only thing he could offer her.

He looked into her eyes—eyes that displayed her soul and mirrored his need. He braced his hands on either side of her face. He caressed her cheek, careful to keep her head steady. "Are you sure you want to know what I want?"

"I wouldn't have asked otherwise." She touched a hand to the stubble on his face and ran two delicate fingers down his cheek. "You count, too, Kane. I wonder if anyone's ever told you that before."

No one had. No one would again. He leaned over and covered her mouth with his. To block out the truth...and to accept it at the same time. Her lips opened and her tongue sought his, not hesitant but eager. She licked his lips, ran her tongue over his teeth, learning and growing bolder with each taste.

He craved her. She was a drug he couldn't get enough of. He threaded his fingers through her still damp hair, then eased his lower body over hers. His arms shook with exertion, from the need to keep a safe distance between them, else he lose control and hurt her more.

Her hips jerked upward without warning. She brushed his erection with nothing more than the flimsy cotton he'd found in her drawer. He exhaled a harsh groan and eased himself on top of her, settling himself between her thighs.

It wasn't enough. He was too damn hard. He wanted to rip off those panties and... A soft moan penetrated the haze of desire. He flipped over fast. Damn but he'd made a mistake.

It wouldn't happen again. Yeah, right. One battle lost, Kane thought, but the bigger war raged on. He rolled onto his side and glanced over. "Are you okay?"

"Too much too soon," she whispered, echoing his earlier words.

He wrapped his arm around her waist and pulled her against him. Once again, his need had gotten in the way of common sense. "Get some rest," he said in a voice rough with unslaked desire, and self-disgust.

"I'm sorry." Her shoulders remained stiff.

"For?" He worked the muscles beneath his fingers, kneading her soft skin. As a distraction, it didn't work. He had a sexy woman in his arms and his body knew it.

"I'm a lot of things, Kane. But I'm not a tease."

"Did I say you were?"

"No. But I'm sure you're thinking it."

He sensed the source of her concern was based in her past and understood. "As a matter of fact, I'm not."

"What are you thinking?" she asked.

That she didn't need to dig into her old insecurities. Not with him. He respected everything about her. "That I pushed myself on an poor, frail, injured woman," he said with a crooked grin.

She laughed. His attempt to lighten the mood had obviously worked. "No, really."

"That I wasn't in the mood anyway."

This time she treated him to a snort of disbelief. "Seriously."

"I was thinking," he said, pausing to smooth her hair and inhale the fragrant scent that was Kayla. "That what just happened..."

"Yes?"

"Was the best almost sex I ever had." Just being with her was beyond good. Kane accepted how much he needed her, even as he knew he'd ultimately let her go.

No matter what emotion and softness she offered him, he'd take none. But for the duration of the case, he'd protect her with his life.

FRESH FROM AN UNEVENTFUL shower, Kayla made her way to the family room. Kane sat staring at the boxes she recognized as holding her aunt's things. "I didn't hear the doorbell."

He glanced over his shoulder. "You should be resting."

She scowled. "I slept half the day yesterday and all last night. I'm fine." Or as close to fine as she could be with the thug's threat still echoing in her brain, her aunt's reputation and her business in jeopardy...and having shared her bed with Kane Mc-Dermott for the past dozen hours.

Like her, he'd showered and changed. Judging by his appearance, she realized his clothes must also have arrived with the boxes. She wouldn't be female if she didn't admit she liked what she saw. Faded blue jeans stretched across his muscular legs. A bleached sweatshirt, navy with white patches that looked as if they'd occurred more by accident than design, covered his broad chest. The detective might not know much about cleaning his clothes but he knew how to wear them. He just plain looked good.

She walked into her family room and knelt down beside him. Her thigh brushed his, a brief and accidental contact. Her stomach muscles curled into twisted bands of excitement and need. What should have been innocent wasn't.

"You've got some color back in your cheeks," he noted.

And it had nothing to do with good health, she thought wryly. "I feel better. Up to tackling those boxes, anyway." She gestured to the opened cartons spread around the room.

"You showered." He fingered her freshly washed hair.

She grinned. "Even I couldn't share the bed with me a minute longer."

"You should have called me."

"So you could stand guard outside the bathroom? I'm not an invalid," she assured him. And she didn't want him treating her as one. His attention was nice, but she didn't want his pity.

"I started without you."

"Find anything interesting?" Her initial inspection of the contents had been cursory at best.

He shook his head. "There're three huge boxes here."

"I packed two of those myself. They lived in an apartment and the landlord wanted it emptied as soon as possible. Economics." She grimaced. "Anyway, Catherine and I gave most of their belongings to the Salvation Army. My uncle had a niece that wanted some of his personal things. Catherine and I boxed the rest to go through later."

"So the crossword puzzles..." His hand settled over the box nearest him.

"Anagrams and things. My aunt loved them. So did my mother. I used to do some when I was younger. I figured maybe I'd get back into them myself one day." She shrugged. "The other box has knickknacks that have been in my family for years."

"How old were you when your mother died?"

The question surprised her. It was as unexpected as it was unnecessary. "Didn't your investigation reveal such a minute detail about my life?" she asked.

"Yes." He had the grace to look ashamed despite the fact he'd merely been doing his job.

"So why ask?"

"Because I like hearing about you from you."

She glanced down at her hands. It was her turn to be ashamed. She'd already forgiven him. She believed what he'd told her earlier—that when he'd slept with her, his job hadn't been on his mind. It had brought him into her life but it hadn't kept him there. When Captain Reid had denied protection, Kane could have walked away. He hadn't.

"What about the business books?" he asked, obviously noting her silence and respecting her wishes by changing the subject.

"I was twenty, Catherine was twenty-one." She answered his earlier question. "It was as if Mama chose the optimal time to let herself go. Neither one of us had to face social services or being separated."

"Wouldn't your aunt have taken care of you?"

"I suppose, but Mama loved us and wanted the best for both of us. Aunt Charlene never had kids and only related well to me because we both had that—" she tapped her head "—extra intelligence, I *guess* you could call it. But she had a harder time with Catherine because they had less in common."

"I'm sorry—for both of you."

She shrugged. "What you lived through was worse." His eyes grew shuttered. His face cleared of expression, almost as if a curtain slammed down, closing out any audience to his soul.

She hadn't reached his inner depths yet, but with time and patience, she would. "I have all the books," she said, accepting his parameters. "That's what's so strange. On the phone, he said he wanted the books. But I've been doing them for the past year. Nothing unusual. No extra income, nothing unaccounted for..."

"They stashed the money somewhere."

Although she hadn't reached his emotions, his words tapped into her own. Kayla grabbed his sweatshirt, desperate for him to understand and believe. "*They* didn't stash anything. Whatever my uncle may or may not have been up to, my aunt wasn't into prostitution."

He met her gaze, his eyes darkening to the color of a stormy sea. "That remains to be seen."

"No. My family may not be as fine as some, but I assure you we draw the line at sleaze."

"I wasn't accusing her...or you. But the fact remains someone wants something from you...and he doesn't much care how he gets it."

"I know." Just the thought of her attacker's voice sent tremors of fear spiraling through her.

Kane grabbed hold of her wrists. His protective warmth eased the terror. "Nothing will happen to you, but we have to find out who these people are and find the books they're looking for. To put an end to all this once and for all."

All this included them. She could read the truth in his eyes and planned to fight it. She just wasn't sure how.

Needing distance, Kayla placed her hands on her jeans and stood. Kane's gaze followed the movement, his eyes traveling the length of her and back. A sensual gleam lit his expression. Swiping a black V-neck Lycra top from Catherine's closet had been a good idea for more reasons than warmth. She doubted her own silk blouses would have elicited the same heated response.

Apparently the trail toward Kane's heart began with sex. Under normal circumstances, Kayla wouldn't offer herself as an object; she'd spent too many years fighting the idea. But Kane was different from other men. For the first time, she intended to use her God-given assets to their best advantage.

"I started with this box," he said. "I figure maybe there's something hidden in one of these puzzle books."

"Like?"

"I don't know yet."

She wanted answers as much as she wanted Kane. Kneeling beside him, each movement she made was deliberate and calculated. She reached inside the large cardboard carton, bending close enough to smell his cologne and far enough over to give him a glimpse inside her shirt...if he cared to look.

She darted a glimpse out of the corner of her eye. He didn't notice her watching him. His gaze was glued to her cleavage, his eyes cloudy, his cheekbones pulled tight.

She suppressed a smile. Despite the less than perfect circumstances and the threat hanging over her, she had Detective Kane McDermott just where she wanted him. The last time he'd *lost his focus,* they'd had sex. And she had every intention of making it happen again. Only this time, it wouldn't be just sex. After she coaxed him into opening up to her, it would be nothing less than making love.

For now, she would tackle what was within her control. She perused each page, smiling as she remembered how both her mother and her aunt would curl up for hours with this pastime. Her mother had been hiding from life. Her aunt had just plain enjoyed the escape. Kayla shut the paperback and laid it on the floor. "Nothing here."

"The ones I've looked through are all completed. Your aunt was an expert."

Kayla grinned. "Easier to be an expert when you work in pencil. Erase your mistakes, cheat a little by checking the back." She laughed aloud. "Aunt Charlene was pretty good. Mama did more cheating than her sister. She made more mistakes, too."

"And you made none at all?"

"I'm not perfect, Kane."

He raised an eyebrow but said nothing.

She glanced at the book in her hand, one that looked like a dime-store crossword, but held precious family memories. "This one's completed, too."

"Let's cover them all. I don't want to miss anything important."

Half an hour later, Kayla wanted to scream. They'd been through more than half the box. The pencil-smudged books were all the same. Most finished, the last few half-finished. She grabbed for the next book in the box. "This is ridiculous."

"Just keep looking."

She curled into a more comfortable position, picked up a pencil and grabbed the next book. This time, she started working the puzzles, much as her aunt had probably done. She chose puzzles and individual questions at random and, just as she suspected, her answers matched Aunt Charlene's. They would, of course, since her aunt had been as intellectual and meticulous as Kayla was.

Gnawing on the end of the pencil, she tossed the book down and went for the next one. Fifteen minutes and three books later, she began finding mistakes. Obvious ones. Ones her aunt would never have made.

Unless she'd done so on purpose. And considering Kayla had also begun finding a pattern of last names in the puzzles, she suspected these were more than game books. The implication of *that* sent chills crawling along her skin, and she groaned aloud.

"Find something?"

She glanced at Kane, knowing she had to reveal her discovery, hating it at the same time. "Mistakes in the entries, names instead of answers," she muttered.

He raised an eyebrow. "Let me take a look."

She handed him the two books she'd made headway with and he scanned the pages along with her notes. "Looks like pay dirt."

She frowned. "Don't sound so pleased."

"It's better than coming up empty."

"What's the date on that first one?" Kayla asked.

"Date?"

"Every book has a handwritten date next to the first puzzle."

"Hadn't noticed," he muttered.

"Marks your progress from month to month, or year to year. Didn't I mention my family was slightly neurotic?"

"No, but you should have. We could have started

at the bottom of the box and come up with something sooner. Come on."

"Where?"

"These books need to be decoded and you need your strength to do it."

"So I can prove my aunt guilty of prostitution and lose my business in the process?" she asked. Kayla might have been ambivalent about putting her dreams on hold for the sake of the business, but she refused to damage her aunt's reputation to get her life back. Aunt Charlene had been the only person other than Catherine who understood Kayla and all her emotional insecurities—because she'd suffered much of them herself. Kayla had no intention of betraying her in the worst possible way.

"So we can exonerate her and save Charmed!'s reputation through you." He glanced down at the first book she'd found with any discrepancy. "This dates back eight months. But Charmed! had been in business for a little over fifteen years."

She nodded.

"Your aunt married your uncle a little under a year ago and took him in as a partner almost immediately."

She didn't question his knowledge. "Yes." Kayla did the math. "The date on the first book coincides with Charles Bishop's entry into the escort business." She heard her voice rising in pitch. "Which gives him opportunity."

"Do you have a reason to suspect the man of anything?"

She shook her head. "Nothing more than sweeping Aunt Charlene off her feet. But the names in these books began around the time he joined the business."

"Which makes him an equal suspect." Kane grasped her hand.

He obviously sought to reassure, but tremors of awareness acted to arouse her instead. He had no right to be so distracting when so much was at stake. "You may have to face the fact that your aunt wasn't an innocent victim," he said.

She shook her head. "Not without concrete, irrefutable proof." The kind of proof she intended to get to exonerate her aunt. She didn't want to believe her aunt's husband had betrayed the woman he professed to love, but better her uncle be found guilty than her aunt. Kayla believed in Charlene.

Kane nodded. "Okay then. We have our work cut out for us."

"We? Does that mean you believe me?"

"Yes."

One little word with a wealth of meaning. She glanced at him for confirmation and found it in the warm blue of his eyes.

"Kayla..." He held his gaze steady with hers. "I believe your faith in your aunt is unshakeable unless we find out otherwise. But I have to reserve judgment until the facts are in."

Kane the cop, Kayla thought. And that was okay. Because hidden in all that qualification was one unmistakable fact: he believed in her. No one other than Catherine or Aunt Charlene ever had.

She didn't think. One minute she was standing beside him and the next she'd wrapped her arms around his neck. "Thank you." She molded her body against his, trying to tell herself it was gratitude. She knew better.

His hands snaked around her waist. If he wanted to push her away, now was the moment, she thought. His grip tightened. The masculine groan and the unmistakable hardness pressing against her told her he wasn't going anywhere, at least for now.

Another second's thought and he might back off emotionally. Kayla recognized her one opportunity to reach inside Kane and make him hers. To do it, she'd have to reach inside herself as well. Take the ultimate risk, and defy every principle by which she'd lived so far. She took two steps back. With trembling hands, she reached for the hem of her shirt. She drew it over her head and tossed the garment onto the floor.

7

KANE TOOK IN THE VISION before him and tried to catch his breath.

Sunlight came in broken waves through the window blinds, bracketing her incredible body in a blazing glow of light and warmth. She inhaled a trembling breath. Her hands shook as she clasped them before her. "Aren't you going to say something?" she asked softly. "Do...something?"

He was no saint. He never had been. Faced with Kayla's offering, he couldn't say no. Her body was too soft, her curves too full, her heart too big. He couldn't turn her away. Even if he burned in hell later.

"Kane?" Even as she asked, she was reaching upward, wrapping her arms around her shoulders to cover herself. From him.

He muttered a savage curse, grabbing her arms before she blocked his view, pulling her hard against his straining body. He held her hands against her sides and looked down at the gift he'd been given, if only for one more night.

He traced the black marks on her throat with his hands. "This never should have happened."

"It's not your—"

He cut her words off with his mouth, sealing his lips hard against hers. He didn't want to hear how she didn't blame him. He didn't want anything except the sound of her soft moans echoing in his ears. He wasn't disappointed.

She responded to his kiss. Her lips softened, her mouth opened, and her tongue darted inside. Wild and unrestrained, she met him move for move. Her back arched, crushing her chest against him until he felt the rasp of hardened nipples through his shirt. Too quickly even that barrier became unacceptable.

He tossed his shirt across the room and then he had what he wanted. He and Kayla, skin to skin, her breasts full, flush against him. He exhaled hard, feeling her softness and heat fuse with him. It wasn't enough, for either of them. She moved restlessly, abrading her nipples against his hair-roughened skin. Her fingers gripped his shoulders. Her nails bit into his skin.

"Make love to me, Kane."

Her voice broke through the haze of desire. Conscious thought intruded. Instead of listening to the pulsing in his groin, he forced himself to think.

He couldn't have sex with her again. Not without consequences. Not with this woman. She broke his concentration and destroyed his common sense. He raised his gaze, forced his lips off the soft skin of her cheek. Her green eyes were fogged with need and more. With emotions he couldn't, wouldn't face.

He ran his thumb over her damp lower lip. "No protection, sweetheart." He felt sure she wouldn't test his resolve by coming up with a box of spare condoms in the bathroom vanity.

"Oh." Shock then disappointment flickered in her eyes. He couldn't stand it. A cold shower would take the edge off his problem, though he knew after last night it wouldn't be damn near enough. But he couldn't leave her hanging, not when he wanted to satisfy her any and every way he knew how.

He wanted to teach her how good things could be between a man and a woman. She'd had little experience, all of it bad. Even he had hurt her in the end. Not this time. Just this once he could give to her, yet still be able to walk away later.

He reached out and cupped his hand around one full breast, letting his thumb brush in rapid motion over her taut nipple.

Her entire body shook in reaction. Had he ever met a woman so soft, so responsive? She exhaled a moan that had his body clenching with need. "But you said..."

He covered her moist lips with one finger. "That I didn't have protection, not that we had to stop completely."

Her eyelids opened wide, comprehension dawning. Before she could answer, he swept her off her feet and laid her down on the couch. At the jarring motion, she groaned aloud. He brushed her hair off her forehead, fingering the still red bruise near her temple. "You okay?" he asked.

"I'd be better if you stopped talking," she murmured, then blushed scarlet at the admission.

He laughed aloud. Kneeling beside her, he placed his hand on her belt buckle. "Good thing for you I'm good at following orders." Especially when he wanted the same thing. Kane needed to see her writhe in pleasure in his arms, to watch her climax beneath his hands. He undid the button and began a downward slide of her jeans.

Kayla helped, raising her hips and shimmying out of the heavy denim. This might not be the result she'd planned, but she had to admit it might be enough. Without realizing it, he'd still given her a measure of control. He seemed more relaxed, less guarded and, best of all, she still had him all to herself.

A phone call to her sister would solve the protection problem later. Catherine wouldn't mind a trip to the drugstore for the right cause. Lassoing Kane was definitely the right cause.

A rush of cool air accompanied the loss of her jeans, but heat quickly followed when Kane placed his hard, hot hand at the juncture of her thighs. A deep pulsing rhythm took hold, starting where his hand pressed intimately against her and traveling to every nerve ending her body possessed. She arched into his waiting palm.

"Damn, but you feel good." His roughened voice caused her heart to trip in reaction.

She forced her eyes open and whispered a prayer of thanks that she had Kane. His own eyelids were shut tight, his jaw clenched. He was as affected as she. Kayla didn't need sex to reach Kane. She could reach him with warmth and intimacy, trust and caring—things she could give him.

She trusted him. She laid her head back against the cushion, prepared to show him how much. As he picked up a sensual rhythm, waves of pleasure washed over her, building, then easing up only to rush her again, more insistent than before. The sounds coming from her throat ought to have embarrassed her, but they didn't. Because this was Kane and the only way he would know how she felt, the only way he'd open up in return, was if he *felt* her trust.

The initial hesitancy of their first night together was gone. The soft moans coming from deep within her shook him as nothing ever had...until her legs relaxed, opening wide, inviting him to continue. Kane sucked in a ragged breath, realizing his mistake. He'd underestimated this woman and her effect on him. Not only was he too damn close himself, but he'd been a fool. He hadn't saved himself by not making love with her. He'd drawn himself in deeper.

He picked up the pace with one hand, easing his finger inside her smooth, wet heat with the other. She gasped aloud. Lowering his head, he drew the tip of her nipple into his mouth and tugged gently with his teeth. That's all it took.

The spasm hit her hard and she arched off the couch. The moist clenching and unclenching around his finger hit him even harder. His own body was close to the breaking point and she hadn't even touched him. He opened his eyes in time to watch her face contort with pleasure *he* gave.

"Kane." His name burst from her lips unexpectedly and the sound triggered an intense reaction so strong, he could no longer remain in control. He straddled her until their bodies aligned, grinding himself hard against her, searching for the fulfillment he'd deliberately denied them both. His unexpected climax took him by surprise. Seconds later, Kane eased himself off her. She couldn't take his weight any more than he could handle what he'd just done. Another battle lost. He couldn't afford to let it happen again.

"That was..."

"Don't say it," he muttered. He'd lost control. Around Kayla, it seemed to be a permanent state.

"Incredible." She turned to her side and gazed up at him with trusting eyes. It was more than he could stand. He started to walk away.

"Don't!" Her harsh tone startled him. "Don't you dare walk out on me."

"You need space."

"You mean you do." She dressed in silence before turning back to him. She ran her fingers through her disheveled hair. "The second you drop your guard, you back off."

He was surprised she read him so well. He shouldn't be. There'd been a connection between them from the minute they met. He raised his hands in a gesture of defeat. "You got me." Kane walked back to where she stood, hands in her front pockets, her expression guarded. He hated that look when directed at him.

He placed his hand around the back of her neck and drew her close. Tasting her lips brought him more pleasure than he could have imagined. Too much. He broke the kiss.

Her dark lashes fluttered upward. "Do I?" she murmured.

He didn't pretend to misunderstand. "Yeah, you do."

Light entered into her green eyes. She looked like a starving cat that had finally found a scrap of food and wasn't about to let go. Of him. Damned if he couldn't get used to the idea—and that unnerved him.

He grasped her chin between his hands. "But don't get used to it, sweetheart." Kane knew he was talking more to himself than to her.

He met her even gaze. The glow in her eyes didn't fade as he'd expected it to. Kayla had obviously decided to take him on and that put him on edge. Her next words proved him right.

"You're used to being alone."

He couldn't dispute that remark.

"But you don't have to be."

She was wrong. Because alone was safer.

Her hand wandered to the front of his jeans. He was hard again, but had no intention of losing control one more time. He reached for her wrist, but instead of pulling her away, he pushed her closer, letting her wrap her fingertips around the heavy bulge in his jeans. He groaned at the absolute perfection he found in her touch.

"Not everyone leaves, Kane." Her whispered words penetrated his thoughts.

She removed her hand, twisting her fingers together in a nervous gesture that revealed she wasn't any more comfortable with the dynamic between them than he was. Sexual tension and an emotional pull. They couldn't deny either. The difference was, she'd obviously decided to take control, to push past her barriers in order to reach him. Which meant he'd made the right decision.

Someone had to keep their distance, to make things easier in the end. "Why don't you go over those books while I jump in the shower?"

"Sounds like a plan." She nodded, ceding control.

Kane knew it was merely a temporary reprieve.

KAYLA WALKED INTO HER bedroom, pausing at the pile of clothes Kane had left lying in a heap on the floor. She liked the casual familiarity the sight implied. Not that she suffered from any delusions that he intended to be a part of her life. That much was obvious.

But she preferred to cling to the hope of the less obvious. The fact that *she'd* taken control and reached past his defenses yet again. She bent down and picked up his shirt and jeans, clenching Kane's clothing in her hands. By the time the case was over, he'd understand the difference between being a loner by choice—or necessity.

And thanks to Kane, she was becoming a woman in charge of herself, and her life. One who no longer feared her sexuality. This wasn't an experience she could regret, no matter what the outcome. But she'd do everything in her power to direct it in her favor.

She tossed the jeans over her arm and something fell to the floor with a thud. Kayla bent down to retrieve his wallet, some spare change and...

"What's this?" Even as her hand grabbed the foil packet and held it up to the light, she knew.

And if Kane went to this much effort to avoid making love to her, to avoid the very intimacy that would enable her to breach his defenses, he had no intention of succumbing. Ever.

She'd been wrong. She hadn't gotten to him. Not even close. She brushed at her eyes before a tear could fall. When had Kayla Luck *ever* affected a man on any plane other than the physical? She should have known better before. She certainly knew better now.

But she had no time for self-pity. She had more important concerns than her love life. Kayla grabbed the five books with possible information and shoved them into an oversize bag. Kane might have directed the course of things so far. But no more.

Kane obviously needed to be shaken up on many different levels. She hadn't been in control sexually, that much was obvious. But there were other ways of taking control and showing Kane there was more to life than being alone.

The mysteries of Charmed! had yet to be unraveled. She could do that without Detective Mc-Dermott. The sooner she did, the sooner she could get back to the life she knew best. Her life without Kane.

She picked up the phone, called Catherine and asked her to meet her at her favorite hideaway. As she replaced the receiver, the shower shut off. The silence echoed in her ears. In minutes Kane would emerge, his dark hair damp from the shower, droplets of water on his skin. She ignored the traitorous thudding of her heart, refused to acknowledge the blood pulsing through her veins. Instead she bolted for the front door without looking back.

KANE WALKED OUT of the bathroom, drying his hair as he went. The silence struck him immediately. His nerve endings, honed by years of experience, went on alert. "Kayla?"

No answer. He didn't call again. His gaze traveled her bedroom. The pile of clothes he'd worn earlier was missing and he realized he heard the hum of the washing machine in the background. But she was gone.

He recalled what happened the last time she'd gone off on her own and his gut churned. She should have known better than to run off. He should have known better than to trust her now that she was back on her feet. Hell, he should have known better than to trust himself. Kayla distracted him in every way possible. His instincts were off, his edge dulled and softened.

He stalked through the house, taking in every detail. Nothing was missing except...the books. He now knew exactly where she'd gone, evidence in hand. A walking target.

Kane muttered a savage curse. When he got his hands on her, he'd throttle her. Never mind that what he really wanted to do was throw her onto the bed and finish what he hadn't allowed himself to do before. "Damn."

He dropped his towel and threw on his clothes, then shoved his feet into his shoes and grabbed for his keys. He had to wrap this case up and get the hell out. He slid into the car, checked his gun and pulled his cuffs out of the glove compartment. The woman drove him to distraction. At this point, he'd cuff her to the damn bed if that's what it took to keep her safe.

THE MUSTY SMELL OF OLD books permeated her nostrils, making Kayla feel safe. She rounded the end of a long aisle and saw Catherine pacing the floor at their allotted meeting place.

She touched her sister on the shoulder. "Hi, Cat."

Catherine turned. "Thank God you're okay. That emergency call scared me to death. Where's your guard dog?" She glanced over Kayla's shoulder in search of Kane.

Kayla shrugged. "I don't know and I don't care." *Liar*. She cared too much, which was what had gotten her into this mess.

"He let you out alone? After he promised he'd

protect you? I should have known the man was slime."

"I snuck out and, if I recall, you liked him well enough the first time you met."

"That was before he took advantage of my innocent sister."

"Don't you think you're laying it on a little thick, even for you?"

Catherine stepped forward and touched her cheek. "You look like you've had your heart trampled and broken. So no, I don't think I'm overreacting."

Kayla eased herself into one of the fabric-covered chairs. There weren't many places in the public library that were comfortable and secluded, but three floors down from the main level, nestled between History and Research, Kayla had carved out her personal space.

"Did you know that men were very literal creatures?" Kayla asked.

"How so?"

"They say what they mean and they mean what they say. If a guy says he doesn't want to get involved, he doesn't want to get involved. No hidden agendas exist. There aren't any fairy-tale endings and there's no such thing as the right woman changing a stubborn man's mind."

"I'd like to strangle the snake."

"Why? He never lied to me. Now sit. We have to talk." Kayla patted the chair across from her. Catherine meant well, but discussing her feelings for Kane was too personal. Kayla wouldn't divulge details, not even to her concerned sister.

She'd cope and deal with it on her own. "What do you know about Charmed!'s less discussed activities?" Kayla asked.

"What do you mean?"

"Look at this." She dug into her bag and pulled out one of the crossword books she'd taken from the house. "Lists of names, dates..." She fanned the pages for her sister to see.

"Shut the book, Kayla." The deep voice took her by surprise. A familiar feeling of warmth curled inside her stomach.

"The iceman cometh," Catherine muttered.

"Shut up." Kayla and Kane spoke at once.

Instead of being insulted, Catherine merely continued undeterred. "What shouldn't she tell me?"

"Anything." Kane's dark gaze bore into Kayla's. If he was aware of Catherine as anything other than another body in the library, no one would know. He had eyes only for her and, if the steely glint in them was any indication, he was furious. She could match and best him on that score.

"Keeping secrets, Detective?" Catherine asked.

"None that concern you." He spoke to Catherine, but his gaze didn't swerve from hers. The intensity Kayla saw there unnerved her.

Catherine's stare bounced from Kane to Kayla and back again. Apparently she sensed the undercurrents running between them because she stood and reached for her purse. "I think that's my cue."

Kayla rose. "You don't need to go." She could handle Kane without Catherine's help, but she refused to let him drive her sister off.

"I think I do. As for Charmed!, I know less than you. Aunt Charlene thought I was the wild child and rarely confided in me."

Despite the seriousness of the situation, Kayla laughed. Catherine never begrudged Kayla her relationship with their aunt. She'd had little in common with the older woman, but Kayla knew in her heart, Aunt Charlene had loved them both. When push came to shove, though, the Luck sisters had relied on each other.

Catherine turned to Kane. "I don't know what the hell's going on between you two, but if you hurt my sister, I'll make you wish you'd never heard the name Luck."

"I believe it," Kane muttered.

"I can't believe you're letting him run you off," Kayla said.

Catherine leaned close, her voice low. "I looked into his eyes. The man's fallen hard. He just doesn't know it yet. He'll take care of you."

"I don't need him…"

"Yes, you do. You're not wearing more fashionable clothes for my benefit, you're doing it for his. Because you finally trust someone enough to let the real you out." Catherine gave her a quick hug. "You know where to reach me."

Kayla squeezed her back. She loved her concern as much as she loved her sister—even if she was seeing things between herself and Kane that didn't exist. In Kane, Kayla had imagined a depth of caring and a need for love in a man who had none. Catherine had obviously been fooled as well. But her sister meant well. They were family and, in Kayla's eyes, that meant everything. Not that a loner like Kane would understand or even care. She glanced over. He stood off to the side, his rigid body language ensuring no one could mistake him for anything but the loner he was.

Despite everything, a huge part of her still wanted to teach him the meaning of belonging. She stifled a harsh laugh, knowing how little he desired from Kayla Luck.

She waited until her sister disappeared around the stacks. "How did you find me?"

"Instinct. You were either here or with your sister. Both happened to be true."

Kayla latched on to his mention of Catherine. "Cat deserves to know what's going on, Kane. Keeping her in the dark isn't your decision to make."

"No," he agreed. "It's yours. The more she knows, the more danger she'll be in. I have enough trouble keeping tabs on you. I don't need to add her to my list."

He took two steps closer. Her personal corner of the library was small. Kane's presence made it seem even smaller. She inhaled for courage and smelled his masculine scent. Her body reacted, recalling more intimate times between them.

Her brain reminded her *she'd* been intimate. *He'd*

been far away. "You can take me off that short list of yours, Detective. I don't want any more from you than you want from me."

"In that case, sweetheart, we're in big trouble."

Her eyes widened. Her lips parted and her breath caught in a noticeable hitch. Kane wanted her more than ever before. He prayed for restraint. "Give me the books," he said, grasping for a distraction.

She shook her head. "I want to work on turning them into a complete list."

"So you brought them here."

"I can concentrate better here."

Away from you. He didn't have to hear the words to know she meant them. Which was no excuse for reckless action. His relief at finding her unharmed warred with his fury at her lack of concern. "You made yourself a walking target."

"This is a *public* library."

Kane glanced around the secluded area. He'd walked down three flights of an empty stairwell and wandered around numerous cubicles and stacks before finding the right one. "Looks pretty damn private to me. And you came here alone, our only evidence could easily have been grabbed."

She cringed.

"Not that I don't think you can decipher these, but I want them in a safe place. I've got a friend at the precinct who's more a bookworm than a cop. He'll cull the information in no time."

"Fine. They're yours." She shoved the books at him hitting him hard in the stomach.

He stifled a grunt.

She grabbed for an oversize bag on the floor. "I'm out of here."

She took two steps. Kane grasped her by the wrist, pulling her against him. He couldn't let her dictate their next course of action. She had no business on the streets alone, but that wasn't the only reason he wouldn't let her go.

Her silken hair smelled of lemons, her skin fragrant and fresh. He didn't just want to keep her alive. He *needed* to keep her alive.

Because that's the way she made him feel.

"Let me go, Kane."

"I can't."

"You already got what you wanted from me."

"You don't believe that."

"I've found a foil packet that says otherwise."

"What the hell are you talking about?" He tensed, unsure of what she meant.

"Don't like being caught?" she taunted. "Then you shouldn't have left your clothes in a pile and I wouldn't have been so quick to help out with the laundry."

"Son of a bitch." His breath rushed out in a hiss. "You're telling me you left the safety of the house, you *risked your life* because..."

"Because I want to control my life." She squared her shoulders. "Besides I don't want your pity, and that's what you gave me earlier. I came on to you and you didn't want me, but you were too much of a gentleman to admit it and make things more difficult, so you..."

"Back up. You think I don't want you?" The thought was absurd beyond belief. He'd never wanted a woman as badly as he wanted Kayla, never let a female get inside and mess with his head before, and that was telling. She was getting to him, a little at a time, taking control and leaving him with none.

He couldn't let it go on much longer, nor could he allow her to think she meant nothing to him.

He turned her around. She had no choice but to face him. Tilting her head with his hand, he forced her to look him in the eye. Shimmering moisture glistened in hers. Damn. His methods of protection backfired in more ways than one. Instead of shielding her, he'd hurt her once again.

His gut twisted with regret and an unfamiliar sense of longing, of caring. He hadn't distanced himself from Kayla as planned, just the opposite, in fact. He was in way over his head.

Reaching into her pocket, she held a black foil packet aloft twirling it between her thumb and forefinger. "I think the evidence speaks for itself."

"Circumstantial, sweetheart." He grabbed her free hand, forcing her palm against the strong erection pulsing against the front of his jeans. "Hard evidence says otherwise."

She sucked in a surprised gasp and Kane watched the play of emotions cross her face. Shock, pleasure and then, ultimately, disbelief. He didn't blame her for fighting the truth. He hadn't given her much of a reason to believe in him. But his body didn't lie and, right now, it strained against her hand.

She tilted her head to one side. Though she met his gaze with a steady one of her own, her eyes showed a range of feeling he wasn't ready to deal with. Wasn't that why he'd left the condom in his pocket to begin with?

"Chemistry, Kane. I read somewhere that men think with their..." Her hand curled around his erection.

He gritted his teeth against the combination of pleasure and agony she caused. "Believe me, sweetheart, I'm not doing much thinking right now."

A heated blush rose to her cheeks. Apparently his innocent Kayla wasn't as comfortable with this situation as she wanted him to believe.

"That's what I mean. So you want me."

"You can feel that I do." His voice sounded rough even to his own ears.

"It's not enough." She jerked her hand back to safety, but the evidence of her touch remained.

"I know." And that was the notion that grounded him. She wanted more than sex. He had nothing more to give.

He plucked the condom out of her other hand. He'd believed that by not actually making love with her, he wouldn't be involved. That by giving her pleasure, he could remain detached. But feeling her wet and warm with his hands, knowing she'd wanted him, had pulled him in. And when he'd gotten out of the shower and thought something had happened to her...

He shook his head. No matter what he felt, Kane knew his limitations. "It's all I can do." He turned the foil packet around in his hands. The crinkling sound echoed in the otherwise silent library.

"I know." She turned a too bright smile his way. "Well, Detective, at least we both know where we stand."

Stalemate, Kane thought. In a war that was far from over.

8

THE POLICE STATION was quiet. Kayla followed Kane inside and waited in the hall while he met with Captain Reid. She didn't need to be in the room while the two men talked strategy. Time alone would give her an opportunity to think and come up with a plan of her own. Between the phone call earlier and the lists hidden in the books, the police had an official case, if not specific suspects to go after. Kayla wanted specifics. With or without Kane McDermott, she wanted her life back.

With her headache beginning to ebb, came the ability to think more clearly. Whoever was behind the attack wanted the books and whatever money they thought she had in her possession. Kayla had read enough to know the bad guys were always willing to swap when they were desperate. She held the books, they held important information. By far, hers was more valuable, which gave her the upper hand.

Before she realized what she was doing, she rose to her feet and knocked twice on Captain Reid's door. Without waiting for a response, she let herself inside. "I have the answer."

"I don't recall asking a question." Captain Reid

rose to his feet from behind the metal desk in the corner.

"Trade-off," she explained. "You know whoever attacked me will call back and when he does, I'll offer him the books."

"In exchange for...?" Captain Reid picked up on her earlier statement.

"Information. I know my aunt was innocent and I want to prove it."

"No."

At the sound of Kane's voice, Kayla turned. He leaned against an adjoining wall in a deceptively lazy stance. The muscles bunched beneath his shirt and his jaw was clenched hard. He glared from beneath hooded eyes. She didn't have to hear him speak to know he wasn't pleased with her suggestion.

"As long as she's willing, McDermott, she's our best option." The older man gestured to the metal-frame chair. "Have a seat."

At least Captain Reid hadn't shot down her idea immediately, despite what Kane wanted. Kayla lowered herself into the chair. "I want my business and my family name cleared." She wanted to feel in control of both herself and her life once more.

Kane shook his head. "Clearing you is my job," he reminded her. One he hadn't done a great job of accomplishing so far. But things were heating up and he was ready. No way he'd allow Kayla to set herself up as a target. "Use a drop or a police decoy."

"In which case we get the errand boy and not the people involved," the captain said.

"I'll lean on him," Kane muttered. "Hard."

"He'll talk if he thinks he's not being threatened." Kayla spoke up. "And what's less threatening than a woman he already roughed up?"

Kane didn't like the enthusiasm in her voice, liked the reminder of the guy's hands around her neck even less. He glanced over, taking in her cheeks flushed with excitement and the determination in her green eyes, and stifled a groan. Back on her feet, Kayla Luck was a force to be reckoned with.

What happened to the quiet woman who liked cozy restaurants, a traveling salesman and books? Even as he wondered, he already knew the answer. She lurked beneath the intriguing woman in form-fitting jeans and a tight, sexy top. A steady rush of adrenaline pumped through his veins. Even this strong-willed version of Kayla excited him in ways he had yet to understand. He'd never run into a woman who challenged him on so many levels. Who dared to assert her authority at the expense of his own. He might respect her independence, but he'd be damned if he'd let her risk her life to get it back. He shook his head. "No meeting. No way."

She braced her hands on her legs and jumped up from her seat. "It's not your decision." She turned to his superior. "Is it?" she asked Reid.

"Ultimately, no."

Kane shot daggers at his boss, but the man

shrugged his shoulders. "The lady asked a question, McDermott. I'm just answering."

Kayla's smile widened. "Then I want in."

"What the hell do you mean, *you want in?* This isn't some action movie, it's real life." Exasperated, Kane ran a hand through his hair.

"Right. It's my life and you guys have shredded it to hell and back. I want to do this."

"There is no *this*." Kane glanced at Captain Reid for backup, certain the older man wouldn't have patience for a civilian plan of action. But he looked more amused than annoyed, which only served to anger Kane more. "No."

"Yes." Kayla folded her arms in front of her.

Despite the serious circumstances, his gaze followed the movement. He took in the press of her forearms against her chest, the rise of her full breasts, visible in the V of her shirt. He knew damn well how that soft flesh felt in his hands, how sweet it tasted in his mouth. He swallowed, but his throat had grown dry.

"Sorry to interrupt this amusing show, but we've got some decisions to make." Reid paced the small area behind his desk. "First, we decipher the books."

"I can do that," Kayla said.

"So can Tucker," Kane muttered.

"Why pull extra manpower on something I can do myself?" Looking too pleased with herself, once again Kayla glanced at the captain for confirmation.

"She's got a point, McDermott. Besides, with you watching her every minute, what can go wrong?"

Kane hadn't mentioned to his boss that he'd lost Kayla for one solid hour because of raging hormones and foolish trust. He wasn't about to do so now.

"And then?" Kayla asked. "What if he calls again?"

"*I* handle it."

She scowled.

"We'll tap your phones and see what turns up," Reid said.

"The last call came from a pay phone," Kane said. He had no doubt the next one would, too.

The captain shrugged. "If he calls, improvise. Go with the moment." He looked at Kane. "You need backup, let me know."

In other words, if the opportunity presented itself and Kayla was still willing, *let her in.* Kane grabbed the bag of books in one fist, Kayla's hand in the other and headed for the door. He knew damn well his boss had a point. He usually did. Kane respected Reid's judgment and looked up to the older man, but he disagreed with his call on this one. Violently disagreed. Kayla might be their best option for ending this thing quick, but he didn't like setting her up as a target. Just the thought made him ice-cold all over.

He picked up his stride. Making his way through the precinct, he ignored the stares of the other cops on duty.

"Where are you dragging me?" She stumbled over her feet in an effort to keep up.

Kane slowed his pace. "Home."

"So you can yell in private?"

There were many things he wanted to do with Kayla. Yelling wasn't one of them. He stopped mid-step and glanced over his shoulder.

She met his gaze with a determined one of her own. "You want an argument, I'm ready. Because you can't talk me out of this."

"I don't want to fight with you, sweetheart."

She narrowed her eyes in obvious confusion.

"Then what do you want?" Kayla asked.

The scene in the library replayed itself in his mind. She didn't think he wanted her. He did. With a need so deep and intense it would have scared him, if he were capable of rational thought around her.

He brushed a soft strand of hair off her cheek. Her pupils dilated at the brief contact.

What did he want? The question hovered between them. Kane knew the answer, just as he knew she needed more. But he couldn't control his need for her any more than he could control the outcome of this case. The most he could do was guide things in the direction he wanted and hope for the best.

He turned to Kayla and answered. "To finish what we started earlier."

OF ALL THE ARROGANT, self-assured, conceited statements, Kane's was at the top of the list. Kayla chopped salad ingredients with more force than necessary, sending tomato juice and seeds flying onto the backsplash against the kitchen wall. *To finish what we started earlier.*

As if she'd allow it without question. Not that she

didn't want to sleep with him again. She did. But that was her body talking, not her mind. A ribbon of warmth curled through her stomach each time he walked into the room. What other proof of desire did she need? However, more important things were at stake than raging hormones. Her life, for one. Her business, for another. And, finally, her future.

It came down to a balance of power, Kayla thought. He thought he could control the situation and her. First by withholding sex. Then, by preventing her from helping to wrap up this mess with Charmed! And now, by informing her she intended to pick up where *they'd* left off earlier. More like where *he'd* left off.

Everything with Kane revolved around his choices and his whims. Well, no more. Someone had to show Kane McDermott he couldn't always be in control. He might not like her plan to uncover her uncle's illegal dealings, but his superior obviously had. Kayla hadn't looked to deliberately thwart Kane, even if that had been the ultimate result. She wasn't looking to be deliberately contrary now, either. But he was about to find out seducing Kayla wasn't as easy as it had been before.

She still wanted to reach him on a deeper level, but she'd been wrong to think sex was the means. He'd ended up taking control of the situation by giving without letting her do the same. He would soon learn that he couldn't control her in bed or out. The detective was about to discover she had a mind and some requirements of her own first.

She added the salad bowl and tongs to the table, set with two places. "Dinner's ready." She called loudly because he'd been dozing in front of the television set in the family room. Neither one of them had gotten much sleep last night, and because they wanted to go through the books tonight, they'd agreed to rest for an hour before dinner. Kayla had been too worked up to rest.

Kane walked into the cozy kitchen she'd decorated with her sister. He'd pulled off the faded sweatshirt earlier. His rumpled T-shirt looked comfortable, slept-in and extremely sexy. He was a man who wore anything well, and her pulse skyrocketed just having him near. Not a good sign, considering she planned to keep a physical distance.

He paused by one of the empty chairs, taking in the kitchen cluttered with pots, pans and cooking ingredients. "I thought we were bringing in."

"And I told you I prefer home-cooked to take-out. Have a seat."

He eased himself into the cushioned chair. "You didn't need to cook for me."

She'd wanted to. As much to vent her frustration over his take-charge attitude, as to get back some semblance of normalcy in her home. She'd also wanted to give Kane a taste of real life, two people sharing a meal and talking over dinner. Since he bolted at the first sign of intimacy, she doubted he'd ever had the experience before.

"I hope you like sirloin." She placed their plates on the table.

He leaned forward in his seat. "This smells great. The last time I had a home-cooked meal was at the captain's house last Christmas."

She could believe that. The man was the ultimate loner. He'd mentioned his mother's suicide but had omitted many details about his father. Kayla didn't think now was the time to ask, but with the right opening, she would.

"I admit I don't have the time to cook all that often, but every once in a while my stomach rebels against take-out. Then I roll up my sleeves and dig in." She cut into her rare steak and juice oozed onto the plate.

She glanced at him, catching him eyeing her plate in barely hidden disgust. "I made yours well-done." At his raised eyebrows, she grinned. "Educated guess. I couldn't imagine you eating anything that still looked alive."

"Good call." He finished his first taste. "And good steak. So why all the fast food? I'd have thought your sister, the cooking expert, handled kitchen duty."

"When she's around, but her school hours and jobs are pretty irregular, so I'm often on my own. Cooking's not my thing. It's hers."

Kane kicked back in his chair, studying her over steepled fingers. "You're very different people, that much I realized immediately."

His lazy gaze zeroed in on hers, causing her body temperature to spiral. The tight top that had felt liberating when she'd chosen it, suddenly felt confining. The heat pumping inside her couldn't be denied or ignored. She wet her dry mouth with a sip of water before attempting to speak. "Cat and I don't share the same passions, but..."

She didn't get any further. His eyes darkened and the word *passion* hung heavy in the air between them. Considering she'd seen him in the throes of that particular emotion, Kayla couldn't mistake the desire reflected in his gaze. Nor did she want to.

Needing control and wanting Kane weren't mutually exclusive. She took a bite of her meal, but didn't taste a thing.

He did the same. "Incredible," he said in a husky voice. He gestured to the food on his plate, but his hooded gaze never wandered from her face.

She felt a burning flush rise to her cheeks. "I thought you were a steak and potatoes kind of guy, so I made...steak and potatoes." She was rambling because his intense stare awakened her desires for so much more than food. Desires she'd promised herself to control until the time was right.

"You seem to know me pretty well," he said.

Superficial information, Kayla thought, and it wasn't enough. She wanted to know more. She shrugged. "Instinct. Something you cops must believe in."

"It's kept me alive more than once."

She smiled. "And now mine is keeping you fed." She pointed to the meal with her fork. "It's not gourmet, but it's decent food." The time had come to push some barriers. "Mama couldn't do more than boil a pot of water, but somehow, we did okay. Catherine's been the cook in the house...ever since the restaurant owner gave her that job to work off the unpaid bill." She glanced at Kane. "So who did the cooking in your house?"

He speared another piece of meat. "I made sure we didn't starve, my uncle made sure we weren't thirsty."

She blinked, not yet comprehending.

"Alcohol, sweetheart. The man guzzled the stuff whenever he got the chance." His face was a blank, uncaring mask.

Kayla suspected he wasn't even aware of the change. He'd had too many years of practice, she thought sadly. "What about your father?" she asked.

He shrugged. "Wouldn't know. He took a hike when I was five. Just like your old man."

She nodded. Though she hadn't known much about Kane's family history, she'd always sensed he'd grown up on his own. Sensed he, too, knew what it was like to be alone. But she hadn't realized how very much they had in common.

At least she'd had her aunt and her sister to give her a sense of family, of belonging. He'd had no one. "It wasn't always easy," she said. "But we got by."

"Same here." Having cleaned his plate when she wasn't looking, he leaned back in his seat. "Your sister might be the chef in the family, but you're pretty good yourself."

Though she appreciated the compliment, she recognized the change of subject for what it was. "Thank you."

"No sweat." He rose and began stacking the dishes.

She shook her head. "I've got it."

"No. You take it easy while I finish up in here. We've got a long night ahead of us."

"The books," she said softly.

His expression darkened. "Yeah, the books." He turned away.

She followed him to the sink, dishes in hand. His shirt strained against the powerful muscles in his back. They'd once rippled beneath her fingertips. She exhaled a sigh. If by a long night, he meant one fraught with sexual tension, she agreed.

His abrupt turn caught her unaware. Suddenly she wasn't faced with the man's back, but his face. His eyes, a turbulent wash of emotions, none of which she could decipher, settled on hers. Razor stubble darkened his cheeks, matching his current mood.

Her fingertips curled around the dish in her hand.

"I want to get one thing straight." He eased the ceramic plate out of her grip and placed it in the sink behind him.

Nothing stood between herself and Kane, no barrier existed between his magnetic pull and her tempted body. Without the small dish in her hand, she felt exposed...naked. "What is it?" she asked.

"I'm here because I have a job to do."

"Tell me something I don't know," she muttered.

"But that doesn't mean I don't want to be here."

Kayla forced a smile. "You want me. I think we've covered this territory before."

"Yeah, I do. But my job means keeping you safe and, despite what I said earlier, that means keeping my distance."

"I didn't know one thing had anything to do with the other." Just twenty minutes ago, Kayla had listed every reason in her mind why she wouldn't sleep with Kane again. Hearing him agree with her, however, hadn't factored into her plan and hurt more than she would have imagined. Now she found herself wanting to argue against her own logic.

This battle of wills they had going was beginning to wear on her. Coupled with the constant sexual pull, the result was a roller-coaster ride of emotions. She wanted the battle to end, but only Kane's capitulation on all levels could do that. He had to trust in her—he had to trust in himself.

Funny, she thought. For years, she'd lacked similar faith in herself. But a few days with Kane, and she'd begun to regain the inner strength and belief she'd been lacking. He did that for her. And regardless of the outcome of *them*, she could never regret the time they'd shared.

But that didn't mean she was about to relinquish control.

"One thing has *everything* to do with the other," he said.

Kayla froze in place. She sensed the import of his statement, understood this was as close a view inside Kane's mind as she was likely to get. So she listened.

"There's something in life called an edge...at least there is in my life. Without it, I'm no good as a cop and even worse as a man. Every time I've let my guard down in any way, things go wrong."

The guilt thing again. She shook her head. "You aren't responsible for what's happened to me."

"That's not what you said earlier."

"You know that wasn't what I meant. I wasn't blaming you."

"Then maybe you should. Maybe both of you should," he muttered.

"Who, Kane?" she asked quietly.

He shut his eyes before speaking. Deep grooves formed at the corners, testament to how difficult this upcoming admission would be. "I always came straight home from school. My mother was fragile, and she relied on me walking in the door at the same time every day. Even before my dad took off, routine was important to her. She got up, washed her hands, ate breakfast, washed her hands, watched TV, washed her hands, I came home, she..."

"Washed her hands," Kayla finished for him.

He met her gaze.

"She sounds obsessive compulsive."

He shrugged. "I guess she was, but I didn't know the clinical term back then. She had good days and bad days, up days and down days." He drew a deep breath. "If I came home from school when I was supposed to, she took her medication on time. And the one day I didn't..."

She walked in front of a moving bus. Kane didn't have

to speak for Kayla to hear. His body shook in reaction to his unspoken words. She reached out and took his hand, silently offering comfort.

The man shouldered more responsibility than was necessary, more guilt than she'd ever imagined. "You said she had good days and bad days, Kane. Isn't it possible she didn't kill herself, but got confused, or wasn't looking? Did she leave a note?"

He shook his head. "Does it really matter? If I'd been home, it wouldn't have happened." His warm hand curled around hers. "And if I'd been thinking about my job and not preoccupied with my feelings for you, you wouldn't have been attacked."

Kayla tried to sort through his words, to hear past his misplaced guilt. He hadn't let go of the boy who felt responsible for his only parent. He couldn't accept it wasn't an eleven-year-old's job to be the adult of the household. While growing up, she and Catherine had borne too many adult responsibilities of their own, and felt an out-of-proportion responsibility for each other. Kayla could relate to Kane's life.

The emotional barriers, the distance, and the all-consuming need to control things around him—they all made a strange sort of sense to her now. She wasn't sure she could ever undo the scars embedded in his past, no matter how much she wanted to.

In the library, he'd told her he was doing all he could do. That had to be enough. When the case was over, if he wanted to stay, she'd welcome him with open arms. If he wanted to walk away, she'd let him go.

He deserved to know he had that kind of freedom.

9

HER TOES WERE PAINTED PINK. Ridiculous he would notice considering she sat deciphering books that put her life in danger. With all quiet for the moment, Kane leaned back in his seat enjoying the view.

She chewed on the eraser head of a pencil, her shimmering lips pursed in thought. Maybe he could take just a quick taste. He shook his head, knowing it wouldn't be enough to lessen the constant ache of arousal, nor would it ease the pressure in his chest that had been present since their earlier conversation.

When was the last time he'd thought of his mother, let alone discussed his past aloud? It had been a long time and he planned for it to be never again. But if soul-baring had given Kayla an explanation for his reluctance to take things further, dredging up the pain had been worthwhile. She'd spent too many years believing herself unworthy of more than an admiring glance or a groping hand. Better she believed *he* had the problem, not her.

Better he walked away from her knowing he'd given something in return.

"Sullivan, John." Her voice brought him back to the present.

"Another big player," Kane said. "He owns real estate all over the city." They'd been at the books over two hours. Rather she'd been at them.

He'd been watching. The shifting of her legs, drawing his attention to the warm place in between. The animation then the scowl of frustration crossing her face, resulting in a pout of her lips that made him desire more than a simple kiss. All in the name of the case, he reminded himself more than once, trying to push aside the things she made him feel.

The first book contained a list of female names that neither he nor Kayla recognized. The women, Kane assumed, who worked for Charmed!'s *side* business. The last few books produced a list of male names as impressive as it was extensive. Where before they only had an informant's tip, they now had probable clients and their call girls. Thanks to Kayla's intelligence and persistence.

As much as he'd fought against letting her handle things, he had to admire the results. He sure as hell admired the woman.

Kane was certain these highly placed, mostly married, men would talk. The more puzzle questions she answered, the longer the list of names had become. They covered all upper-crust walks of life. And none of these men would want the scandal sure to be caused if their private lives were made public.

"I need a break." She stretched her legs out in front of her. Bare feet peeked from beneath narrowed blue jeans and she wiggled her toes in a long stretch.

"Put it away for the night. You've still got the end of a concussion and need rest." Something he wouldn't be getting much of tonight. After spending the evening watching her work, that much he knew for sure.

"Don't I know it. Besides, except for one last run-through, I think I'm near finished." Her eyelids fluttered closed, shades of exhaustion evident. "But I have to finish tonight." She grabbed for the first book in their pile, the one that began the list of names, and fanned through. "We have a growing list, but we're no closer to...Kane?" Her voice rose in excitement.

He sat forward in his seat. "What is it?"

"Major change here. I don't know why I didn't notice it before. Look. All the earlier books were done in pencil, right?"

He nodded. Not that he'd have noticed if she hadn't pointed her family's quirk out earlier. Experts at crosswords did them in pen with no fear of mistakes.

"But here—there's a mix of pencil and pen." She studied the book for a second and grabbed another, glancing through it. "This one, too. Look."

He was beside her in an instant.

"Here. Black ink instead of pencil. I don't know why I didn't notice it first time around."

"I missed the change, too." He skimmed the pages of the remaining books. "Same with these."

"This is it, Kane. It's what I was looking for. It's my aunt's clue."

"What?"

"It was her way of letting us know she wasn't doing this willingly, Kane. I'd bet my life on it."

He closed his eyes at the thought. He was getting damn tired of her life being on the line. She didn't need to remind him. "Okay, let's say you're right."

"I *know* I'm right. When the guy grabbed me the other day, he mentioned money and when he called he mentioned the books. *These books.*" She drew a deep breath. "Not only do they have the names, which is incriminating enough, but maybe he knew Aunt Charlene was dropping clues."

"Possible," Kane muttered.

"So tell me why we can't find a trace of the money," she said with frustration.

"There're plenty of places to hide cash without the accountant knowing," he said. "Offshore accounts, for one. Without a number they're untraceable."

"But this guy seems to believe I know where the money is. Why?"

He shrugged. "Impossible to know what they're thinking. But they do want their take. Any clue in those books where the money could be hidden?"

She shook her head. "Just the names. No phone numbers, either, since these are all letter puzzles."

He shrugged. "The money is something we might never find. Unless things unravel well at the end. My guess is the men in those books contacted someone at Charmed!, not vice versa. Too risky the other way. Your uncle probably took the calls."

"My uncle?" A grin edged the corners of her luscious mouth. "That means you believe me—Aunt Charlene was being used or threatened."

"Like I said, anything is possible, sweetheart. But the lists are extensive. At the very least, she knew what was going on." He hated like hell to remind her, but he didn't want her hurt more in the end because she hadn't considered the possibility.

She folded her arms across her chest. "That doesn't mean she was a willing participant. I believe she had no choice."

Kane didn't know what to believe other than the fact that Kayla believed in her aunt. Hell, he didn't blame her. If he'd had even one person to rely on in his life, he wouldn't want to give up hope, either.

He glanced at Kayla. He wanted to believe in *her*. But his job required proof. They didn't know what the change from pencil to pen meant. Maybe they never would.

She wasn't ready to count the older woman out yet. Kane groaned, wishing for her benefit she wasn't so naive. And yet that was what he loved about her...

Kane coughed.

"Are you okay?"

He forced a nod and mentally changed topics. "Whoever these clients contacted, they probably paid cash, your uncle supplied the women, took his share and cut his partner in on the rest."

"The man we want."

"Or woman," Kane reminded her. "Remember the Mayflower Madam, for starters."

She nodded. "They also want the books, which means *these* books." She lifted one in her hand.

"Your uncle's leverage," Kane said. "With these in his possession, your uncle was guaranteed his take."

She glanced at her watch. "It's been hours since the last call."

"It's a waiting game. The more time that goes by, the more nervous you'll get. They hope."

"Well, they're right. I'm more than nervous. Just the thought of what could have happened, terrifies me."

"You've realized how dangerous it would be to get even more involved." Fear released its hold. He exhaled a rush of air, the first easy breath since she'd announced her plans in the captain's office hours earlier. "Don't worry. Reid won't mind," he went on. "We can work around it, use a decoy. Just remember, when he calls, keep him talking. Maybe we can trace it. Agree to a drop, not a face-to-face meeting and—"

"I haven't changed my mind." She interrupted his instructions in a soft but determined voice.

"But you just said..."

"I admitted I'm afraid. I'm human. So sue me. But I haven't changed my mind."

"If you're shaky, it'll show. Things could get messy. Go with your gut."

"I am and my gut tells me I have to do this."

"Dammit, *why?*" He slammed his hand against the end table beside his chair until it rocked on unsteady legs. He'd roared. She didn't flinch. Not a sign he was even close to convincing her to opt out.

"Look." He braced his hands on his legs and leaned forward in his seat. "There are experienced people to do this for you. No risk. Why not take advantage?"

She ran a hand through her hair. The soft strands fell back around her face, creating a vulnerability he knew was part real, part illusion. This woman was tougher than the softness on the outside revealed. It was just a part of why he was drawn to her.

"It's my life that's been turned upside down and *I* want to be the one to get it back." She met his gaze. "Like you, I've been taking care of myself longer than I can remember. It's not in me to give up the job to someone else, even when it gets tough."

"Dangerous," he countered.

"Whatever."

"You'd be relinquishing the job to professionals. There's a difference."

"Not to me. I gave up a decent job, with a decent salary and dreams of finishing school to run this *family* business. Because, despite it all, I love my family. Now I find out it might be a front for an escort service. Am I the only one who doesn't miss the irony here? I have to see this through to the end. And I have to clear my aunt's name."

In her voice, Kane heard the same determination he felt on every case. In her eyes, he saw the same need to accomplish a goal. He respected it enough to want to know more. "Just what *irony* are you talking about?" he asked quietly.

She rose from the couch and crossed the room until she stood beside him. Her scent worked against his restraint, tantalizing his senses, seducing his soul.

"It's proof," she whispered. Meeting his gaze, she lifted her hand, then let it drift downward, boldly outlining the rounded swell of her breast and the generous curve of her hips. Her nipples pressed taut and rigid beneath the cream-colored T-shirt she'd changed into before dinner.

His mouth grew dry, his palms damp. Wanting Kayla wasn't new. It was as much a part of him as breathing. But right now, it was damned inappropriate. His brain registered the fact his pulsing body seemed determined to ignore.

With great difficulty, and even breathing, willpower won out. "Proof of what?" he asked in a hoarse voice.

"This." Her hand traced her curves once more. "This is an illusion."

"A beautiful one." One that tormented him on a minute by minute basis.

Thinking back to their first meeting gave him a clue as to what she meant now. He recalled her inability to accept a compliment and her immediate withdrawal whenever he stared too long, or got too close. He'd gotten past those barriers, but not without effort.

He glanced at the body made for sin. "But it's not what counts," he said.

"You're the first person to recognize that." Appreciation lit her gaze and a warm smile lifted her lips. The knowledge that he could touch her on such a fundamental level pleased him.

"You're the first person to see beyond the bimbo."

He winced at her coarse put-down of herself.

"It's one thing for me to run a charm school. Another for someone like me to take over what turns out to be an escort service or worse. I mean, look at me. The girl from the wrong side of the tracks, the girl they couldn't vote most likely to do anything, because they believed she already had. Of course, she and her family are behind a prostitution ring," she said with a brittle laugh.

Kane would like to go back in time. To beat the living daylights out of anyone who had even looked at her sideways. And if they had the nerve to put a finger on her body, or let her name pass through their lips...then he'd like to...

She reached upward. Her fingertips traced what had to be a scowl creasing his forehead, then she smiled. "Don't look so fierce." Her voice was lighter now. "I grew up hearing it. Words can't hurt me anymore."

Her steady green gaze zeroed in on his. She pinned him in place with a searing look. "But lack of faith in me, in my abilities, can. *You can.*"

He didn't need an interpreter to understand. He'd just been suckered by the intelligent woman beneath the well-rounded curves. He'd been taken in by the best.

Kane shook his head. He had to admit, he was impressed. He'd never run into someone who could hold their own with him, let alone best him without much effort. He hated and respected her involvement with the case, all at the same time. Should he continue to fight her determination by opposing her plan, he'd be no better than the scum who came before him. Men who'd looked at the body and assumed Kayla was easy.

Kane knew better. She challenged him. She intrigued him. And though she'd not only enticed him but seduced him on many levels, Kayla Luck was far from easy. Caught in a trap of his own making, he had no choice but to support her, back her and make damn sure he did his job.

No mistakes. No distractions allowed.

HER SHOWER FINISHED, Kayla puttered around the bedroom. The sun had set and only the small light of a lamp illuminated the room. She fluffed her pillows, then sat down on the edge of the mattress. Alone.

Just outside the closed door, she heard Kane prowling around the kitchen. Though she lived with her sister and was used to the sounds of another person in the house, Kane's presence lent a different feel. Anticipatory. Intimate.

She glanced at her nightwear choices laid out on the bed. On the one hand, the washed football jersey Kane had picked out for her the other day. On the other, a frilly negligee stolen from Catherine's drawer.

Choices. How many times since she'd met Kane had fundamental decisions come down to two drastically different choices? To seduce or not to seduce. To...

The jarring ring of the doorbell startled her. She clipped her damp hair off her forehead, yanked on the lapels of her robe and started for the door.

She didn't get far before Catherine's voice sounded loud inside the house. "No lectures, Detective. I have a right to clean clothes."

"Ever hear of a washing machine?" Kane asked.

"I'll be out of your hair in less than five minutes." Footsteps sounded in the hall and drew closer. "Make it ten. I want a visit with the prisoner."

Kayla laughed aloud. A talk with her outspoken sister was exactly what she needed, too. Enforced confinement with Kane was getting to her, making her lose perspective. She only hoped a dialogue with a biased third party didn't complicate things even more.

She opened the door at the same time Catherine pushed from the other side. Her sister stumbled in. "Well." She paused in the doorway. "At least he doesn't keep you locked in."

The sarcasm was for Kane's benefit, Kayla knew. Catherine had already given Kane the Luck seal of approval. Her sister just didn't want the man to get overconfident and cocky. No chance of that, Kayla thought. Cat didn't realize Mr. McDermott didn't want or need to be a part of their little family.

"He couldn't keep me locked in even if he wanted to." She slid the bobby pin out of her hair. "Contingency." Kayla grinned.

"See?" Catherine tilted her head and glanced over her shoulder. "I taught her well, McDermott. If you want her, you'll have to work for it."

Kayla grabbed her sister's wrist and yanked her inside, slamming the door before Kane could reply. "Are you insane?"

"Just keeping him on his toes," Catherine muttered. "Something you should be doing. I come here figuring I'm going to interrupt some hot sexual encounter and instead I find you in your bedroom, dressed in a ratty robe, and him on the other side of the house, slamming cabinets and muttering to himself."

"So that's why you rang the bell."

"I can be discreet if I have to." Cat flopped down on the bed. "Now tell me why I didn't have to." She laid her hand down on the mattress.

Kayla cringed as her sister's fingers curled around the silk and lace garment she'd borrowed. "Hmm. Now things get interesting. I guess I jumped to conclusions. You don't need my advice after all."

"Wrong," Kayla said. "Get up."

Cat frowned. "Why? I'm comfortable."

"Get up."

Catherine rose and glanced down, then picked up the large shirt she'd sat on seconds before. Her eyes opened wide and she groaned. "Honey, you've owned this rag since we were teenagers. It's fine for hanging around with your sister, but won't do jack to seduce a man."

A vision flooded Kayla's mind...of wearing that same shirt when Kane kissed her, moved over her, then came as close to burying himself inside her as possible considering the physical barrier their clothing provided. Slick warmth trickled between her thighs at the memory. Then came another vision. That of Kane easing himself off her when he remembered she'd been injured and wasn't ready, of him holding her throughout the night in comfort. This was a man who could make her both writhe in pleasure, and relax in contentment, in his arms. A potent combination.

"Earth to Kayla." Catherine waved a hand in front of her eyes. "I don't know where you were, but it's obvious you've made the right choice." She picked up the leopard print and black lace garment, dangling it from her fingertips.

Cat's style, Kayla thought. Not hers. A smile formed on her lips. She felt it. She welcomed it. Things between herself and Kane were sensual, hot...and honest. She didn't need sexy clothes to attract his attention. If she'd learned nothing else over the past few days, she'd learned to accept herself— her heart, her mind and her body.

She had Kane to thank for opening her eyes, for empowering her in ways she'd never been before. If she wanted to, she was perfectly capable of enticing him on her own—without the teddy. *If she wanted to.*

The issue in question wasn't what she should wear to bed...but whether or not she ought to invite Kane to join her. By virtue of his silence, he'd conceded his end of the power struggle where the case was concerned. He would support her decision to participate in wrapping up the case on *Charmed!* Agreed against his better judgment because he believed in her. But he didn't like it and was concerned about protecting her, about keeping the edge that made him effective as a cop.

She loved him too much to jeopardize his career...their future. *She loved him.* Heaven help her.

Despite all the planning and effort to remain in control where Kane was concerned, she'd failed miserably. She'd fallen in love with the loner detective, which meant she was without a safety net now.

Her entire future hinged on Kane's past. And if things didn't go well when she met with the man who'd attacked her, Kane would hold himself responsible, just as he did with his mother. In that case, she had no doubt he'd walk away without looking back.

She didn't delude herself. She might lose him either way. But she believed in odds, and she intended to stack the deck in her favor. To regain control in whatever way she could. She grabbed the lingerie from her sister.

Cat smiled wide. "Whew. I feel better." She glanced at her watch. "Five minutes are up. The warden's going to come knocking any minute." Leaning over, she gave Kayla a quick hug. "I'll just grab a change of clothes and get out of your way."

"Take care of yourself, Cat. This mess isn't over yet."

"I will. You know that. And you do the same." She walked to the door, pausing to glance over her shoulder. "Let the seduction begin," she said with a grin.

"Bye," Kayla murmured. The door shut behind her sister. Kayla glanced at the garment in her hand, fingering the luxurious silk before burying it in the back of her dresser drawer.

She didn't need clothes to seduce the man, but she intended to do everything in her power to make him realize what he'd be giving up should he decide to walk away.

HE COULDN'T HANG OUT in the kitchen for the rest of the night. Besides, it wasn't doing him any good. Kane had sat through Kayla's shower. Listened to the pulsing, pounding rhythm of the water while his body throbbed to the same beat.

He'd envisioned the stream of water sluicing over her curves, the beads of water clinging to her skin. He braced his hands on the counter and exhaled a groan.

"Something wrong?"

His insides twisted even more at the sound of her husky voice. He turned. Kane didn't know what he expected. A sexy siren, a vixen to match the arousing voice? He could have handled her and in an absurd way she would have been preferable to the down-to-earth woman facing him now. The old football jersey wasn't sexy, but the garment had its own share of memories. The faded sweats were far from revealing, but the effect on him was the same.

She looked warm and welcoming.

He *felt* warm and welcomed. Two sensations he'd never experienced before, at least not in conjunction with a woman. "What are you doing here?" he asked.

"I live here," she said wryly. "And I was cold after my shower. I figured something hot to drink would take care of that."

She joined him by the counter. The lemony scent of her shampoo clung to her hair, bringing temptation to life. "Coffee?" he asked. "I saw some instant in the cabinet."

She shook her head. Damp strands of blond hair clung to her cheek. God, he wanted her. "Tea?" he managed to say.

Her smile caused a tightening in his gut.

"Not what I had in mind," she said.

"What then?"

Without answering, she reached for the handle on the cabinet behind him. Her arm brushed his shoulder. The heat struck hard and hot, where it counted most. Her touch was electric. He inhaled and counted to five until a semblance of control returned.

"Hot chocolate always seems to do the trick...when I'm cold." Her voice had dropped an octave. The husky sound turned the knot in his stomach even tighter.

She met his gaze. In her eyes he saw a deadly combination of uncertainty and longing. Kane had been around long enough to know when he was being set up, that she was grasping to regain control. But Kayla's seduction, or attempted seduction, wasn't like any other. It was an endearing mixture of innocence and sensuality. One he couldn't withstand no matter how much he needed to.

He'd already drawn the line and Kayla knew it. He was certain she'd respect his decision to keep his distance, if only because he'd accepted hers to participate with Reid on closing the case on her business. But she was playing a dangerous game with him now, tempting him, hoping he'd give in...wondering how far he'd let her go before backing off.

He wasn't sure himself. Around Kayla, his self-control was minimal. His only choice was to turn the tables and hope she chose to retreat first, instead of advance.

He stepped toward the refrigerator to her left. "Would you like some whipped cream on top? I seem to remember you enjoy it." Reaching for the handle, he brushed his forearm across her breasts. The barrier of her clothing might as well have been nonexistent as the hardened peaks of her nipples rasped across his bare skin.

She exhaled a slow moan. He grit his teeth against the arousing sound and the pleasurable feel of her breasts against his arm. His jeans, already too snug, were now damned uncomfortable. He turned toward her, trapping her between the counter and the length of his body. Her body heat called to his, her scent beckoned to him. Kane wondered when he'd begun to enjoy torturing himself without mercy.

He glanced down. She gripped the sides of the cardboard box of instant cocoa mix, denting the box with her grip. At least she was affected, too.

He leaned forward. "Whipped cream, Kayla?" Her eyes darkened, remembrance and desire flickering in the depths.

"I..." She swallowed hard. "I don't keep any around. It's fattening, and I have to draw the line somewhere, I mean there's only so much indulgence a person can take and..."

"Tell me about it," he muttered. Kane reached out and eased the box from her hands. Her breathing now came in shallow, uneven gasps. He wasn't doing too well himself, but damned if he'd let desire rule his head.

Time to end this game before it got out of control, Kane thought. "Relax, sweetheart." He touched her reddened cheek with his palm. She tipped her head into the cradle of his hand. Such an innocent gesture. One that nearly sent him soaring out of control.

He inhaled hard and fast. "You look flushed. Is your head okay? Maybe your blood sugar dropped. Have a seat and I'll make you something to drink." He wrapped an arm around her waist and led her to the nearest chair. It had been too long since she'd taken any kind of break.

Having changed the subject, he exhaled. His breathing came easier, but not much, considering her soft curves now molded against him...and he was strung tighter than ever.

The next move was hers. Kane was counting on it. She had no choice but to take his cue and move on...unless she wanted to end up tangled between the sheets. And though they both *wanted*, they each had their own agenda as well. She'd let it go, he told himself again.

She stopped short of sitting down. "I'm not thirsty anymore. I think I'll just go to bed, instead." He released his next breath in a whoosh of air. She'd accepted his boundaries. He wouldn't be getting any sleep tonight, but at least he was back in control.

She stepped backward, tilting her head until she looked him in the eye. "Ready?"

"For?" he asked warily.

"Bed. Aren't you going to join me?"

He muttered a curse. Where this woman was concerned, control was a goddamn illusion. What made him think he had any power or control over a situation where Kayla Luck was involved?

Just one more reason he had to put this case, and her, behind him as fast as possible. But he had to get through the night first. "I'll take the couch." He crossed his arms and waited for her next shot.

Kayla shot him an amused glance, aware that Kane was edgy and uncomfortable. And it was thanks to her...and the idea of sleeping with her. Amazing.

When in her life had she had the ability to put a man like Kane on the spot? When had she ever made any man feel awkward? Maybe it was an ability she'd always had but never had the courage to explore before. With Kane, she felt secure enough. Comfortable enough. She liked that feeling.

Almost as much as she liked him. A smile formed on her lips. "Go ahead, sleep on the couch. But I should tell you, it's lumpy and uncomfortable. You won't get much sleep out there."

"What makes you think I'll get any sleep in there, with you?" He gestured toward the hallway and her bedroom.

"Because I'm tired, still injured, like you said." She slicked her hair behind her ear. "And besides, I don't recall inviting you to do anything else besides sleep."

His eyes darkened under lowered lids. "You invite a man into your bed, sweetheart, you better be prepared for anything." Need echoed in his voice.

Her knees went weak and her insides turned to jelly. Another second and her mind would follow. Then lust would take over and she'd lose everything. Reaching out, Kayla grasped his hand, intertwining their fingers together. His skin felt rough and warm against her palm, his hand felt right in hers.

She'd grown up feeling as if she had to fight for everything that mattered, from her mother's attention to accepting the adult she'd become. Even a business she'd legitimately inherited had turned into a struggle she might not win. Nothing had come easily, some things not at all.

But Kane, her love for this man, mattered more than anything else ever had. She'd fight for it, so that when the end came, she'd have no regrets. None she'd have any control over, anyway. She tugged lightly on his hand.

"Don't do this." His voice held a ragged warning.

She refused to listen. "I've got used to sleeping in your arms, Kane. Is that so much to ask?"

10

THE CLOCK ON THE nightstand read midnight. Kane glanced at the woman lying beside him. Her even breathing told him she was asleep. Damned if he could say the same. How could he when lying beside Kayla, breathing in her scent and sharing body heat had begun to feel familiar? To feel right?

Add to that the fact that she wanted him, too, and nothing was stopping him from waking her up by easing himself inside her. Nothing except his own damn sense of right and wrong. Control was no longer an issue. Kayla's feelings were. As soon as this case ended, he was history. So why hurt her more than he already had?

Rolling to the side, he levered himself to a sitting position. The bedsprings creaked beneath his weight as he stood. Kayla didn't move.

He walked to the window and rolled open the blinds. A full moon lit the night sky and its glow streamed into the room.

"Kane?" The rustle of sheets followed the sound of her voice.

He turned. "I didn't mean to wake you." Or maybe he had. He'd begun to hate being alone with only his thoughts for company.

She turned back the covers on his side. "Come back to bed."

Did she know what she was asking? His body churned with need. If he climbed back into that bed, it wouldn't be for sleeping.

She curled her legs beneath her. "I'll tell you a bedtime story." Humor tinged her voice as she patted the sheets with one hand.

How could he resist an offer like that? He eased himself beside her. He wrapped an arm around her shoulder and she settled against his side. "What was your favorite?" he asked. "Sleeping Beauty? Cinderella?" He named fairy tales he'd only heard of thanks to the recent VCR releases advertised on TV. He sure as hell hadn't been on the receiving end of bedtime stories while growing up.

"The Ugly Duckling," she murmured.

He tangled his fingers in the short strands of her hair. "I should have known."

She yawned. The vibration caused his body to come alive. "Why's that?" she asked.

"Because, like that duckling, you turned into a beautiful swan."

She shook her head.

"Yes." He rolled onto his side so he could face her, then cupped her cheek in his hand. "You're beautiful."

"No, I'm..."

"Yes, you are. Now say, 'Thank you, Kane.'"

Even in the muted light, he could see the blush stain her cheeks. "Thank you, Kane."

He grinned. "Call that lesson number one on how to accept a compliment."

"I didn't know I needed lessons."

She did. Desperately. She'd made progress since they'd met, but she wasn't there yet. Maybe one day she'd stop fumbling over the subject of her looks or her body. But he wouldn't be around to see it...which meant someone else would.

Was that what he was doing? Kane wondered. Priming her for the day when the right guy came along? That was a thought worth blocking out and he knew just how to accomplish his goal.

Leaning over, he brushed a kiss over her lips. He wanted to tune out his thoughts and black out the future. He wanted a harsh, demanding kiss that wouldn't let him think or feel. Unfortunately for him, Kayla wasn't cooperating.

She was kissing him, but setting her own pace and speed. The control issue had returned and it was all hers. Light kisses on his mouth and delicate whispers of her tongue over his lips let her tease, play and arouse. But worse, gave him time to think. About how much he wanted her, desired her and how great his need for this woman always seemed to be.

Her hands splayed against his chest. The warmth of her fingertips penetrated his skin. Heat of a different kind pounded inside him, insistent, demanding release.

"Kane." Her lips moved against his.

He traced the line of her jaw with his tongue, ending by tugging on her delicate earlobe with his teeth.

She moaned aloud and her fingertips curled into his chest.

"Kane, no."

"No?"

"No." Kayla lay back against her pillow, out of breath and obviously out of her mind. What other explanation could there be for stopping him, when she wanted him inside her more than she wanted her next breath? But she could handle not making love with Kane again—barely. What she couldn't handle was the regret he would feel after they made love because he'd given in to emotion and lost his focus once more.

He exhaled a groan and rolled over to lie beside her. His muscular leg straddled hers, and through the cotton briefs, his rock-hard arousal pressed hot and heavy against her thigh.

Her stomach muscles clenched with desire while the dampness between her legs begged her to reconsider. She couldn't. She had too much respect for him to change her mind.

"You said you wanted to keep your distance." She used his own words as a deliberate barrier between them. She hadn't meant to play the role of a tease, rather she was gambling for her future.

"Guess I changed my mind."

"Your hormones did. Your mind, your heart..." She tapped lightly against his chest. "Those things haven't changed."

"Can't argue with reason."

"Guess not," she whispered. Though she'd

wanted him to do just that. Still Kayla had known it wouldn't be easy.

He stretched an arm around her and she curled into him. "It's okay, Kane."

"What is?"

"I stopped before you did something *you* would regret, but you have to know…it's not something *I* would regret."

"Are you saying you changed your mind?" His hands tangled in her hair. It was a habit of his, she realized, one she enjoyed. The erotic tugging against her scalp turned her on.

No doubt that's what he intended. "No, I haven't changed my mind. I'm still respecting your original decision. But I want you to know something else." She paused, in the space of a heartbeat. "I don't expect anything from you. When this is over, you can walk away without looking back. I won't stop you."

The ring of the telephone shattered the ensuing silence and spared him having to answer. She glanced from the digital clock to the phone. "No one I know would call at this hour." The persistent ringing continued.

He clenched his jaw. "Answer it."

She picked up the phone. "Hello?"

"I'm through playing games, lady."

Her hand went to the bruises on her neck. "Is that what you were doing?"

Silence greeted her on the other end. She looked at Kane. "Keep him talking," he mouthed and edged closer.

"I...I have something you want," she said into the phone.

"You ready to start up again?"

The question startled her. She hadn't expected him to make that kind of suggestion. She avoided answering. "I'm ready to turn over whatever I have to... Who did you say you work for again?"

The gravelly laugh on the other end sent chills racing through her. "Lady, I'm no dummy. This isn't about work. My mother's sick. She wants the crosswords your aunt used to do. The ones she bragged about. I'm sure they'll keep a sick old lady busy."

"I have them."

"Tomorrow, noon. Ditch the boyfriend and be at The Silver Café." A click sounded on the other end.

"Not enough time," Kane muttered.

"I tried."

"I know." He eased the phone out of her hand. Her fingers ached and she realized she'd been gripping the receiver way too hard. Just like the fear that gripped her heart. But she could handle this. She had to handle this.

"What else did he say?" Kane caught her shoulders with both hands.

His touch steadied her. She forced even breaths into her lungs and replayed the conversation in her mind. "He knows about the crosswords, that my aunt was responsible for those. And he wants to meet tomorrow, at...at..." Realization dawned. "He's been following me."

"What makes you think that?"

"He wants to meet at the restaurant you took me to. That's not a coincidence. I've never been there before you. I didn't even know the place existed. He said to ditch you and show up alone. How does he know about you? How long has this guy been watching me?" Her voice rose along with her hysteria.

"Kayla." Kane shook her gently. "Hey. He's just trying to rattle you."

"Well, he's done a good job."

"Then back out. No one would blame you and I sure as hell would welcome it."

"You know I can't." She met his gaze.

"Then don't let him win. Don't let him make you think you aren't safe." He drew her into his arms. His warmth enveloped her, his strength supported her. "Because you are."

KANE DIDN'T KNOW HOW LONG he held her. Only that at some point, they lay down on the bed until her breathing steadied and relaxed. The first time he tried to untangle their legs, she resisted. He must have dozed off because the sun now shone through the window where moonlight had been.

He called Reid from the kitchen phone. His boss answered his home line on the first ring. "Meeting's on," Kane told him. "Noon today." Kane didn't like it, but he had no choice.

He'd given up all leverage where Kayla was concerned. She'd cut him loose and he hadn't argued. Even if the phone call hadn't interrupted them last night, he wouldn't have fought the point. She'd given him his freedom, something he'd had anyway, but for some reason, she thought he needed her permission to walk away.

She'd been clear on that point. She didn't want anything from him. Though it was exactly what he needed to rid himself of any unwanted guilt, the thought rankled. *Why the hell didn't she want more?* And why the hell did he care?

"Hey, McDermott. You wake me up to breathe into the phone or you want to discuss backup?"

Focus. A little after noon today, he'd have that ability back in spades. "Yeah, boss." Kane gave details about Kayla's phone conversation. "The meeting is at the same place the department sprung for dinner the other night. It's crowded at lunchtime, so I'd just have some well-dressed undercover cops drop in for a meal and make sure I'm in the booth behind them."

"No deal. If he followed her the night you two did the town, he'll spot you in a second."

The captain was right, but damned if he could just send Kayla off on her own. "Either I'm there, or the meeting's off."

Reid should have come down hard on him for asserting authority. He didn't. His harsh laugh echoed across the phone lines. "If I didn't know better, I'd say you were after my job, McDermott."

"I'd rather rot than sit behind a desk," Kane muttered.

Reid laughed again. "Okay, just keep out of sight. Make sure she hands over the books and opts out of the partnership. He takes them, we move in. That's it."

"I'll coach her. She won't even breathe at the wrong time."

"Yeah, I trust you to be on top of things. Are you ready to end this?" Reid asked.

Kane knew the older man meant more than the case. He'd switched into paternal mode. Reid didn't do it often, but Kane appreciated the attempt. Too bad he didn't have an answer that would satisfy either one of them right now.

KAYLA FISHED THROUGH HER closet for the third time. Silk blouses, linen slacks and sensible pumps. Had she really expected the contents to change just because she had? Even during the days she'd worked nine-to-five as an accountant, wearing corporate suits and stuffy blouses, she hadn't altered her wardrobe on weekends or days off. She was lucky she owned even one pair of jeans, considering she'd had no desire to wear them.

Until now.

Until Kane.

There was no way she wanted to walk out of this house looking like the woman he'd met three days earlier. Not when she felt so different inside. Raiding Catherine's closet was the only solution. A few trips to her sister's room and she'd made her decision. She pulled a pair of black cowboy boots over her jeans, then eased another of Cat's V-necked tops, this one a buttercup cotton, over her head.

Glancing in the mirror, she ran some styling gel through her hair, when she caught site of Kane standing guard in the doorway.

"Ready for action. How do I look?" She turned toward him.

His scowl spoke for him. "This isn't a date. What the hell do you think you're doing, dressing like that?"

She recognized his roar. She'd gotten to him on some level that made him uncomfortable. Mission accomplished, she thought and smiled. "I'll take that as a compliment. So you like it?" She smoothed the oversize top down over her hips.

"Damn right I like it. You look great." His smoky gaze lit on hers.

Her grin widened. "Thank you, Kane," she said with a deliberate lilt to her voice.

The tension eased and he smiled back. "So the files were right. You are a quick learner."

"I'm the best."

"I know that," he muttered. "Now take it off."

"Excuse me?"

"You don't want to arouse the guy, you want him in and out as fast as possible. You want to convince him you want out of the business, not that you're looking to be hooked up with his next client."

"Jeans and a cotton top, Kane. It's standard dress for most women."

"You're not most women," he muttered. "Now do this one thing for me. You don't want *that* kind of reaction from the guy."

"I didn't think." Not about anyone's reaction to her outfit but Kane's and she'd already gotten that.

"That's the point. You're taking this whole meeting too damn lightly."

"If you're talking about the clothes, I'll change."

Kayla wasn't one to argue with reason, no matter how bossy the command sounded. Besides, this was her golden opportunity. Her one chance to have Kane see he could be emotionally involved without harmful or, worse, fatal repercussions. Everything rode on this meeting turning out as planned. She would follow his advice, but she would also show him that she could stand on her own.

"But if you're talking about attitude, you ought to take a lesson. Will obsessing over it change the outcome? You prepped me and I'm ready. I'll be wearing a wire and I know you'll be as close as possible. I'll be surrounded by protection."

"And you don't move from your seat. Either he wants the books or he doesn't. You got that?"

"Considering you told me at least ten times, how could I forget? Relax, Kane. Take a lesson from me." After her initial panic last night, she'd realized nothing would alter fate...whatever it held. Somehow, the knowledge eased her fear and helped her remain calm. "I can't control the future," she told him. "But I can enjoy *now*."

He threaded his fingers through hers. The comfort she found in his touch amazed her, as did the strength of her feelings. She'd only known him a short time, but it was enough.

"Is that what you're doing?" he asked. "Enjoying now?"

"What else?"

"Changing before my eyes." He tugged on her hand and she drew closer. Their bodies aligned until she felt his weight and heat pressed intimately against her. His arms wrapped around her waist, moving her into the V of his legs. His erection hardened and grew against her stomach. A harsh groan escaped his lips, telling her he was unbearably aroused.

At that moment she knew she could have one last time with him. *One last time.* His hips jerked forward and she swallowed a moan. She licked her dry lips. "You tempt me, Kane."

"Only fair since you drive me out of my mind." His lips lowered, capturing hers. This kiss wasn't urgent and out of control, it wasn't slow and determined with seduction as the result. His tongue delved and played inside her mouth, devouring, arousing...remembering for the future.

Kayla had no doubt. In Kane's mind, this was goodbye.

SHE ORDERED A DRINK from the waiter, as planned. Kane breathed a sigh of relief. He'd heard her loud and clear through the wire she wore. Now he settled in to wait.

Five after twelve and the lunch crowd had all taken their seats, fellow cops with big appetites and good instincts. He'd still rather be inside himself rather than eavesdropping from the manager's office just outside the dining-room entrance.

"It's time." A male voice interrupted Kane's train of thought.

"Actually past time. I've been waiting since twelve, like you said." The edge in Kayla's voice was unmistakable. *Relax, sweetheart.*

"Change of plans. I can't stay long."

"Too bad," Kayla said. "I...I just ordered a drink and I was hoping you'd join me."

Perfect, Kane thought. Keep him talking and keep him in the restaurant. Kane leaned forward in his seat.

"Not that you don't tempt me, honey. You do. Hell, with a body like yours you'd tempt a monk, but I'm in a rush, so...maybe some other time."

"That might be possible if I wanted to continue the business—which I don't."

"I don't know what you're talking about. Like I told you on the phone, my mother's sick and I want some of your aunt's crossword books to keep her busy."

Damn. The guy suspected a trap. Kane hoped like hell Kayla stuck to the plan. "Give him what he wants," he muttered.

"You know, my aunt was really into these books. I'd hate to just give them to someone who didn't appreciate them the way she did. I'm sure you understand." Kane could practically see her batting those big green eyes for effect...at the same guy who'd wrapped his arm around her neck without a second thought.

He exhaled a groan. Though she was doing a great job of attempting to exonerate her aunt, and things seemed to be going smoothly, this whole mess couldn't be over soon enough to suit him.

"Your aunt liked to play games," the man muttered. "And apparently it runs in the family. My mother's not too sick to play them herself."

"Well, good. Just tell me how involved my aunt was in those games and you can take the books back to your sick mother...with my best wishes for a speedy recovery."

"Not here. I've got a car waiting outside. You walk me to it and I'll tell you all about how much my mother and your aunt had in common."

Remember the plan, Kane thought. Hand him the books and sit tight. Given no choice, a smart middle-man would take them and run. Kane had already promised Kayla they'd lean hard on this guy and anyone else he ratted out to discover the extent of her aunt's involvement. She didn't have to jeopardize her life for her aunt's reputation.

"I'm sure you can make the time for one drink." Her voice was practically a purr by now. Only Kane recognized the hint of desperation and fear within.

"Not a chance. Let's go."

"Hand him the books," Kane muttered through clenched teeth. Instead he heard the slide of a chair against the floor.

"Just let me grab my bag," she murmured.

Kane slammed his hand hard against the wall, ignoring the immediate swelling caused by the impact against concrete. Sweat began a steady trickle down his back.

He wanted to run into the hall and tackle her to the ground to stop her. But then he'd blow the case for sure. There were strategically placed cops outside, she'd be fine. She'd be fine.

The guys had wanted to shoot hoops after school. Kane couldn't because he had to get home to his mother. "One game, McDermott. Ten minutes. No big deal." He'd never said yes before, but the guys were insistent. Ten minutes turned to thirty, then an hour passed. Kane hit the streets at a dead run. She'd be fine, he'd told himself. She'd be fine.

"There's the car. Now I'll take the books." The man's voice snapped Kane out from the grip of old memories.

"Fine. But I'm done. I have nothing to do with this end of the business. I want to be left alone."

That's a girl. Too late for Kane's piece of mind, she was out there with less coverage than before. But at least she was sticking to the rest of the rules he'd laid out while he was wiring her earlier.

Now if the guy would just attempt a clean break, and if Kane's people could move in, they'd be all set. If, if, if... Dammit why couldn't she have stayed inside?

"That's a dangerous proposition. Just ask your aunt..." The man's laughter mixed with the hacking cough of a long-time smoker. "That's right, you can't and you want to know why? She never wanted to be involved and look what happened to her."

"It wasn't an accident." The horror in Kayla's voice caused Kane's heart to twist into a tight knot.

He shook his head, feeling her pain like his own. *You were right all along about your aunt's innocence, sweetheart.* And Kane should have trusted her gut instinct as much as he trusted his own. Because he l...

A car horn blared in the distance and her attacker's voice sounded next. "I didn't say that, but if thinking it keeps you in line, I'm all for it. Now hand over the books."

"You killed Aunt Charlene." Shock tinged Kayla's voice.

Dammit, hand over the books.

"The books, lady."

"Ouch. Dammit, okay. You're hurting me," Kayla muttered. "Here."

A loud masculine grunt followed. Kane recalled Kayla nearly doubling him over with the same books and couldn't suppress a half-laugh, half-groan at her unmitigated gall.

Without warning, the sound of a lone gunshot rang out, shocking him as it echoed in his ears. Kane bolted for the door without looking back.

11

"YOU DON'T SHOOT WHEN a civilian's involved."
Kane's shout reverberated through the air, stopping
passersby on the street.

"You do when there's a safe shot," the rookie re-
torted.

"Didn't you learn anything at the academy? There
is no such thing and I'll make sure you have plenty
of time to remember that while you're walking the
beat for the next month."

Kayla cringed from her perch on the curb where
she'd fallen. Some trigger-happy cop had decided to
take out the suspect when he'd tried to drag her into
the car along with him. She supposed she should be
grateful, but from the anger in Kane's voice, she
knew they'd both be paying for the foreseeable future. If Kane even stuck around that long, now that
they had the guy in custody.

The rookie had hit the man in the leg and he'd
dropped hard, his weight taking her down with him.
Now he lay moaning in pain, surrounded by police.

"And you." Kane rounded the circle of cops, his
attention now fully focused on her.

The adrenaline rush from seeing him was much
more potent than anything that had come before. His

intense gaze settled on her face and her heart rate kicked into high gear.

"I thought I told you to stay put. To make sure you didn't leave the restaurant. But following orders isn't in your vocabulary, is it?" He loomed over her. Big, powerful and sexy, despite his all encompassing anger.

Her fingertips curled around the curb and the rough concrete bit into her skin. "Not when I'm stranded on my own and forced to improvise. He said move, I moved. I didn't think…"

His jaw clenched in a gesture she'd come to recognize, one that signaled the calm before the proverbial storm. "You're damn right you didn't think. You didn't think he'd grab you, didn't think he'd try to drag you into his car, didn't think some rookie looking for a promotion would see his chance and fire."

She'd put herself in danger while he was powerless to stop it…just like with his mother. Kayla realized the foundation of his anger way too late to prevent the flood of emotion she'd inadvertently unleashed. The yelling came from deep concern, and fear of reliving his painful past.

"I'm not hurt, Kane."

"But you had to push him," he continued as if he hadn't heard. He probably hadn't. "You had to know about your aunt. You couldn't trust me to do my job…" His voice trailed off and he paused, shaking his head. "It's not like I gave you any damn reason to."

Kayla shook her head. She trusted him, all right.

With her life and with her heart. But he wouldn't believe her any more than he'd want to hear the truth. Because Kane was only concerned with his job, not with emotions he hadn't asked her to feel for him. This turn of events hadn't helped. In fact, that rookie had probably shot her happy ending to hell and back.

Kane had wanted a neat wrap-up, no problems, no proof that he'd let his feelings sway his judgment in any way. Life had just thrown the unexpected in his path. He'd have to deal with that, Kayla thought. The man had emotions and it was past time he got in touch with them.

She quickly cataloged her body and not finding any overt injuries, she levered herself to a standing position. Unexpected pain shot through her ankle when she put pressure on her foot. She forced what she hoped was an easy smile. "I'm fine."

His hand reached out to stroke her cheek. Spiraling dizziness assaulted her. Not from the shock of the past few minutes, but from his heated touch and the caring it implied.

"You just winced." His husky voice shook her composure. Could she dare hope he wouldn't be able to walk away?

"Did I?" She shook her head. "I didn't realize. That guy weighed a ton and I took the brunt of his fall. Look, Captain Reid's here," she said, hoping to distract him so she could walk the kinks out of her ankle.

Kane placed his hand on the small of her back,

waiting for her to precede him. She drew a deep breath and took her first step. Her ankle buckled beneath her.

His muttered curse coincided with the sudden weightless sensation of being swept off her feet.

"What are you doing?"

"Getting you the hell out of here."

She gripped his shoulders with both hands and held on tight. Hard muscles flexed beneath her fingertips and an accompanying rhythm began to hum inside her as well. She couldn't suppress a shiver of desire. "Put me down and let me walk on my own. This is humiliating." And arousing. And it felt way too good for something destined to end.

"Captain."

The older man walked toward them.

"Anything you need from her you've got on tape. She'll be down tomorrow to make a statement," Kane said.

Reid nodded. If Kayla wasn't mistaken, an amused smirk clung to the edge of his mouth.

Embarrassment flooded her. She could only imagine the shade of pink that probably washed over her cheeks. "I can walk," she muttered in Kane's ear.

"You heard the lady, McDermott."

Kane shook his head. "She's got a choice. X rays at the hospital or ice at home until I know if there's swelling."

Though she should be used to it, Kayla bristled at his take-charge attitude. Still a tiny part of her reveled in the attention, probably because there wouldn't be much more in her future.

Her heart clenched in denial. "I'll take the ice at home." At the very least, their goodbye would be in private.

KAYLA'S FREEZER LOOKED about as empty as Kane's apartment. The place he called home. The place he'd be returning to tonight, alone. He slammed the door closed hard.

"Don't take your anger out on the appliances. I can't afford new ones," Kayla yelled from the couch in the next room.

"I can't find an ice pack," he called back.

"That's because, despite how many times I've been hurt this week alone, we're not accident-prone around here. There are plastic bags in the top drawer. You can put some ice cubes in there."

He popped freshly made cubes into the clear bag and joined her in the room she called the *family* room. Ridiculous word, he thought. It conjured images he wanted to run from. Visions of sitting beside Kayla in comfortable silence, of warm sheets, and confidences...of their legs tangled together in her bed. Leaving her wouldn't be easy, but he had no choice. She deserved better than him and, Lord knew, he didn't deserve her.

She'd propped her ankle on a double set of pillows. After checking out the swelling, he realized it wasn't nearly as bad as he'd first thought. A bad bruise at the very worst. Still a little first aid couldn't hurt so he laid the ice on her elevated foot.

A shudder rippled through her.

"Cold?" he asked.

She nodded.

He could warm her. The thought hovered unspoken, but the need to act on it was clear. Selfish, but clear. One minute he was kneeling on the floor by the couch, the next he was lying prone beside her—and not easily. The narrow cushions weren't made for two.

"It's cramped, but I like it," she said.

He'd been around her long enough to recognize the sensual undertone. The unintentional but blatant desire in her voice touched something inside him, probably because he recognized the same longing in himself.

"I'm warmer now," she murmured.

"I know." Shared body heat had never felt so good. Her breath blew softly against his cheek and the swell of her breast pressed against his arm.

Before he could enjoy the sensation, his weight began a slow descent off the sofa's edge. He caught himself before falling and jerked his hips back onto the couch.

Her husky laugh reverberated through his already tight body. "Your choice, Kane."

He respected her for that. The days of power plays were over. He hadn't planned a return to this house, but then he hadn't counted on things playing themselves out the way they had. In the split second before he'd hit the street, he'd had a flash of Kayla lying sprawled on the pavement covered with blood. A scene he'd seen once before with a different end. She was alive, though, and offering herself to him.

A blatant invitation he could accept or decline. An invitation with no strings attached, because as she'd so boldly told him, she didn't expect anything in return. Selfish bastard that he was, he couldn't turn her down. He needed her too much. One last battle lost before he waged his final campaign. He glanced toward the front door, knowing his last battle was one he could not let himself lose.

Before gravity could pull him back toward the floor, he shifted his weight so his legs straddled her hips. The weight of him pushed against the V of her legs with unmistakable pressure and she moaned her pleasure. The sound twisted his insides in coiled knots only she could undo.

He reached for the buttons on the prim and proper shirt she'd changed into earlier at his urging. She'd already removed the wire on the way home. Keeping his eyes on the road had been damned near impossible, but he'd managed. Barely.

He worked at the buttons with shaking hands, reminiscent of his first attempt as a teenager in the back seat of an old beat-up thing his uncle had called a car. The only difference was this wasn't nerves causing the problem, but overwhelming desire that could no longer be restrained.

"The hell with this," he muttered. He grabbed the sides of her shirt in each hand and pulled.

Little pearl-like things popped and scattered in myriad directions. Kayla gasped. Kane looked down, and his breath caught in his throat. Her cleavage swelled above the lace border of her bra, while her nipples stood erect against the white material. He brushed each distended peak with his thumbs. She sucked in a ragged breath and her hips jerked involuntarily beneath him.

Catching him by surprise, she reached out and grabbed his shirt in her fists, pulling him down and easing him over her. He didn't wait for her next move, but captured her mouth in a kiss as possessive as it was desperate. And wasn't that what he was? What he'd been since the day he'd met Kayla Luck? Desperate for her love and acceptance, knowing he could take neither?

Her rounded breasts pressed flush against his chest, molding to his body as if she was made to lie against him like this, be with him like this, forever. Before he could react to that thought, she kissed him back, her tongue sweeping inside his mouth, in an act of possession all her own. She did what nothing else could—she distracted him, stopped the thoughts rolling in his head that told him he had to leave, until he could think of nothing but her. Until he was filled with her feel, her touch, her scent.

Her lower body mimicked the slick motion of her tongue as she writhed in frustration against the barrier of clothing still separating them. Her fingers, still gripping his shirt, curled tighter and pinched his skin. Without warning, her body began a violent trembling. She was obviously near the edge, as desperate as he was to join together on one last ride.

"Kane." She spoke his name into his mouth.

"Hmm." He raised his head and stared into the gorgeous green eyes that would stay with him always. "What is it, sweetheart?"

"My foot's numb."

"Huh?" That was the last thing he'd expected to hear.

"The ice. Get it off my foot," she said with a frustrated laugh, shaking her injured leg in an obvious effort to dislodge the pack. "Please."

He grabbed for the plastic bag with one hand.

"*Ahh.*" She drew the word out in a long, satisfied sigh.

He laughed. "And here I thought it was *my* place to make you sigh with pleasure...but if it's ice that works for you..." He opened the zipped seal and reached inside. "Far be it from me to deny you." He held one melting ice cube over her chest.

Her eyes opened wide, watched as he traced the outline of lace with the cold block of ice. He eased the cube back and forth, pausing only when water accumulated, to lick the droplets from her soft skin. Her eyes glazed with pleasure and need. The sounds coming from the back of her throat aroused him like nothing else could. His body screamed in taut agony, begging for release.

She grabbed for his shirt, this time pulling the edge from the waistband of his jeans. He helped her pull the shirt over his head and toss it onto the floor.

But when she made a grab for his zipper-fly, Kane paused. He wanted to let her continue. He wanted to shuck his jeans, remove hers and finish what he'd just begun.

But that was the point. He'd just begun. If this was their final time together, he wanted it to last.

His fingers were damp with water and a small cube remained in his hand. He traced her full lips easing his finger inside her mouth and leaving the ice on her tongue. The kiss that followed was erotic and hot, a mixture of ice-cold and Kayla's warmth. He nearly came right then.

But the bag wasn't empty. With the last ice cube, he went back to the drawing board. He cupped her full breast in one hand and followed the pattern on the lace cup with the other. She groaned, then laid her head back on the couch in obvious submission. He took his sweet time, circled her breast with excruciating slowness. Each turn brought him closer to his goal, to the hardened peak at the center. At that last touch, her back arched and only his hips kept her anchored in place.

She raised her head and met his gaze. "Games are over, Kane."

"Believe me, I'm not playing any..."

"Yes, you are..." She licked her damp lips with her tongue. "And they're finished. Not that I'm not enjoying them, but control time is over."

He shouldn't be surprised she knew his intentions before he'd even figured them out himself. She read him well; she always had. Right now he didn't care and wasn't about to argue. He wanted her so badly he shook with it, he needed her so much he ached.

At that moment, Kane knew, he'd probably ache for the rest of his life. But not Kayla. She'd get over this, get over him. Not a thought he wanted to entertain now.

He paused only to remove the last articles of clothing that separated them, then swung one leg over her already parted legs. His touch found her damp and wet, waiting only for him. Bracing his hands on her outer thighs, Kane drove himself home.

HER SKIN WAS STILL tingling from where the ice had touched her flesh. Her heart was still beating in overtime from the intensity she'd found in his arms. Kane had done everything she'd dreamed of, and some things she hadn't.

He'd lost control. Ceded a part of himself to her in passion. How ironic that in the giving, Kayla knew she'd lost him.

They dressed in silence, like the two strangers they'd once been, not the friends and lovers they'd become. But she'd made a promise and she intended to hold herself to it. *I don't expect anything from you. When this is over, you can walk away without looking back. I won't stop you.* Time to respect her own words...even if her heart was breaking.

He pulled his shirt over his head and tucked it into his jeans. The rasp of the zipper echoed in the awkward silence.

He turned toward her. "If the ankle swells, you'll call..."

"I'll call a doctor," she reassured him. If he was going to leave, the least he could do was get out quick.

He nodded. "Good. You can use ice tonight..." His voice trailed off. Just the mention of the everyday item caused ripples of sensual awareness to prickle over her skin. Kayla rubbed her hands up and down her arms, but the chill remained. She supposed she'd have to get used to the feeling.

She rose from the couch, careful to keep the pressure off her injured foot. She wanted to face Kane for the last time standing and poised, not hobbling like an invalid. He was great at caring for the needy. The last thing she wanted was to be the victim who needed his protection once more.

The many facets of Kane McDermott made sense to her now. Not that the knowledge could change things.

In Kane's mind, each case brought the chance to redeem himself for failing his mother, for failing himself. Remain in control, don't lose focus—those were his mottos. And most especially, don't give anything up emotionally...because if he did, he risked repeating the past. If he loved, he risked losing again. Kane had been closed up for too long to take that kind of risk now.

Kayla knew it from firsthand experience. Each time he opened up, the old fear gripped him and he shut down again. She glanced at the rigid set of his jaw. He'd shut down now.

She couldn't fight the past for him. She'd just come through fighting her own. As a result, she had no choice but to let him go.

"Don't forget to come down tomorrow and make your statement."

She sucked in a harsh breath. She'd forgotten she wasn't through dealing with Kane on all levels yet.

His expression softened. "I'll be making mine tonight and I'll be off all next week. Reid will take good care of you."

Obviously he'd read her mind. She shrugged. "Whatever. If *you're* finished taking care of me, would you mind just..." She gestured to the door, an excuse to swallow the lump in her throat. "Just go, Kane. It won't get any easier."

His curt nod was abrupt, his features schooled into that damned unreadable mask he'd perfected over the years. If only she hadn't seen him laughing...or in the throes of passion...she might not hurt so badly right now.

He stood beside her. His hand reached out to touch her cheek. "If you need anything..."

She drew a deep breath. His unique scent enveloped her, making her feel warm and cherished. An illusion, she reminded herself. "I won't."

He nodded and withdrew his hand. His gaze met hers once more before he turned and headed for the door. The bleakness she glimpsed in his eyes betrayed him, but she knew better than to think he'd act on his feelings.

"Bye, Kane."

The door closed behind him. A silent goodbye. She had to admit, the man was good. Too good, she thought and turned to clean up the remnants of living with Kane McDermott.

"IT'S BEEN A WEEK SINCE we swept the underworld," Reid said. The older man rounded Kane's desk and took a seat across the way. "And what a week it's been." He kicked his feet on top of the aging, dented metal and exhaled a grunt of satisfaction.

"You always were modest, boss." But in this case Reid's pride was understandable. For all Kane's concern over Kayla's welfare, not once had he considered the possibility that Charmed! had been tied to organized crime. No one had. The signs weren't there.

But Kayla's uncle had been a small-time operator looking to make it with the big boys. He'd taken all the risk and cut them in on a huge profit in the hopes of proving his loyalty. He hadn't counted on his wife, Kayla's aunt, getting cold feet. She'd threatened to turn over the books she'd been keeping as insurance to the police. As a result, both had met their untimely ends. The remaining key players in the scheme had counted on the very thing Kayla despised. They figured the *bimbo* niece in need of cash would play ball, and business would continue as usual.

She'd been in more danger than anyone realized at the time. The realization still had the power to churn Kane's gut and turn him ice-cold. The thought of Kayla haunted him twenty-four hours a day. Erotic dreams caused tossing and turning at night and softer memories left him unfocused during the day.

"Let me gloat, McDermott."

Kane shifted his attention back to his boss.

"After all these years I've earned it. I'm this close to retirement..." Reid gestured with one hand. "And I never figured on going out on a case this big."

Kane laughed at the excitement in his superior's voice. "As soon as he heard the words *murder charge*, our pal spilled names, dates, hits—cases we never thought we'd solve and guys we never thought we'd nail."

Reid grinned. "Amazing what the promise of the Witness Protection Program will do to a guy's sense of loyalty."

"He was loyal," Kane countered. "To number one."

"And what about you?"

Kane stood, shoving his seat backward so hard the chair hit the wall. "What the hell is that supposed to mean? You're questioning *my* loyalty?"

Reid didn't flinch. "Not to the department, no. But to yourself? Yes."

Kane groaned and eased himself back into his chair. Father-mode had obviously kicked in again. "Tell you what. You worry about retiring on a high, and I'll worry about myself."

"Will you? I don't think you've given a crap about yourself since the day your mother walked in front of a moving bus."

Kane didn't question where he'd gotten the information. His life was an open record to those who needed to know. But Kane never spoke of his past aloud. Not to anyone...except Kayla.

Reid might have taken a fatherly interest in Kane, but Kane had never confided personal specifics in return. "If you were anyone else, I'd slug you for bringing that up," he muttered. And if he'd been feeling anything like himself in the week since he'd walked out on Kayla, Kane might have shut the old man down anyway.

But he'd been a walking miserable, bleary-eyed son of a bitch. He figured hearing Reid out couldn't hurt. Hell, at this point, it just might help.

"Have you seen her?" Reid asked.

"Who?"

The captain rose from his seat. "Know what, McDermott? I have to meet the D.A. for lunch and I don't have the time to play who's dumber with you. You want to live life alone, the way you have been, go right ahead. You want to let her walk out of your bed and into someone else's..."

"Hey."

"Hey, what? I just told you I'm through playing who's dumber. You win that award hands down anyway." Reid braced his hands on the desk. "The lady makes you a human being, McDermott."

"Go play footsie with the D.A. I don't need this crap."

"No, but you need *her*." Reid straightened. "By the way, you did a hell of a job on this case, Kane." The older man's voice softened. "You called it as something before even I believed the lady needed protection, you kept her safe and coached her good. I'm proud of you, son."

Kane's mouth grew dry. Before he could answer, Reid disappeared out the station door.

CLOSED. At least temporarily. Kayla flipped the sign on the inside of the door so the word faced the busy street. Charmed! was no more. Kayla and Catherine had sold out.

"What next?" Catherine asked.

"Beats me. Your tuition is paid in full for the year, so that's not a concern."

She frowned. "It is to me. If I'd known back in September how this would turn out..."

"You'd have taken the money anyway. I have a career to fall back on. Now you will, too."

"Accounting?" Catherine scowled. "How can you even consider going back to number crunching after all the changes and excitement in your life?"

"Excitement is overrated," Kayla said wryly. Excitement meant Kane, and he was gone. Time to move on, she thought, no matter how difficult. Despite how it sounded to her sister, Kayla didn't intend to fall back into the old Kayla mode. Not for long, anyway. "Accounting is practical and it'll pay the bills."

"The sale of the business will pay the worst of the bills until we get back on our feet. Accounting isn't you. It's the woman you were before all this." Her arm swept the expanse of the room. "It's the woman who wore trousers and buttoned-to-the-collar silk blouses..." Cat's voice trailed off as she caught sight of Kayla's outfit.

The black knit slacks and the light blue silk top had been the least offensive things in her closet. "I own one pair of jeans, Cat. They were dirty. Cut me some slack."

"Only if you go shopping, and soon."

"When I can afford it," she reminded her overindulgent sister. They might have made a small profit on the notorious business, but there were loans, bills and other necessities that made frivolous spending impossible.

"I can take a leave of absence from school, we can get back next semester's tuition..."

"Not a chance. You'll finish."

Silence reigned for all of thirty seconds. "Okay. I'll cook, you'll count, until the school year is finished. Then we switch. I make the money, you go back to school."

Kayla shook her head. "School, books, language degrees...I'm tired of those things. I just didn't realize it until..." *Kane.*

Her sister smiled and tilted her head in a sympathetic gesture Kayla recognized immediately.

"Don't worry about me, Cat. I'll be fine."

"I know. And as long as you're free for the foreseeable future, I have an idea I want to run by you. For a new business. A catering business. We'll start small and offer every kind of service imaginable—decorations, hors d'oeuvres, serving, catering, party-planning—we can use what's left of the money for start-up costs." She paused for breath. "And eventually I'll get to use my cooking skills full time while your talent for organization will keep the business going. We'll target small parties at first and then try for the bigger clients once we establish a reputation. I thought..."

Kayla laughed. "Slow down, Cat." She shook her head at her sister's enthusiasm, though she had to admit she liked the idea of planning parties instead of crunching numbers. "It sounds ambitious..."

"But you love it. And get this name. *Pot Luck.*" Catherine emphasized each word with her hands. "Slogan, We Meet Your Every Need."

Kayla rolled her eyes. "I think our family's already been down that route."

"So capitalize on innuendo and imagination. We weren't involved. Heck, you made headlines bringing down the mob."

"You're exaggerating."

Catherine laughed. "Yeah. But I made you smile for the first time all week—since that lousy son of a bitch betrayed my faith in him and walked out."

"He did what he had to do." Kane hadn't gotten past losing his mother or his supposed role in her death. Kayla had spent much of the last week at the library researching psychology books on suicide, the people who remained and guilt complexes. Many of the articles she'd read described Kane's withdrawal and resulting pain perfectly.

The knowledge didn't take away her regret or loneliness, but it did help her to understand the man she'd loved and lost. Kane had never let go of his guilt, anger and fear. He probably never would.

"You're too forgiving." Catherine picked up the letter opener on the desk. "Personally I'd like to slit his throat...or that other part of his anatomy. The only part he was thinking with when he..."

"Enough. He doesn't deserve it. I'm dealing without Kane just fine."

"Say that enough times and maybe I'll believe it. Better yet, maybe you'll believe it. He hurt you, and you have to acknowledge that. At the very least, vent and you'll feel better."

"Is that why you're twirling a letter opener in your hand and issuing empty threats against Kane? To get me in touch with my feelings?"

Cat grinned. "Whatever works."

The bells over the shop door tinkled, distracting her attention. Sunlight gleamed through the doorway and the front windows, blinding in its intensity.

"Afternoon, ladies."

Kayla shut her eyes against the harsh glare...and the sound of the deep, familiar voice. She was dreaming again, just as she had been last night, awakening with her clothing damp with sweat, her thighs tingling from an erotic, sexy dream starring...

"Isn't someone going to speak?" Kane asked.

"You'd better be here to grovel because I'm not about to let you hurt her again."

"Good to see you, too, Catherine."

At the sound of their bickering, Kayla opened her eyes. Kane stood inside, leaning against the bookshelves on the side wall, out of the sun's glare. He'd entered, but his wary expression told her he was by no means sure of his welcome. He might be uncertain, but he wasn't unsure. Power and sexuality oozed from every delectable inch of him.

His penetrating stare shifted from Catherine to Kayla. "Do you want me to leave?" he asked in a controlled voice.

Her heart squeezed tight in her chest. Of course, she didn't want him to leave. Yet how could she subject herself to any more pain? Whether she heard what he had to say now, or asked him to leave later, the result would be the same. He'd pick up and go. His intentions had always been clear. She'd just been too stubborn to heed them.

Kayla exhaled, knowing she had no choice. She loved him enough to hear him out, even if it was just department business that brought him. The thought nearly suffocated her.

She turned to her sister. "Catherine, I think you should go."

Catherine shrugged and headed for the desk chair

where she'd deposited her coat. "Your choice. I just hope he proves himself worth it."

Kane glanced over Cat's head to meet Kayla's gaze. "Is she going to be this tough for the rest of my life?" he asked, a grin edging his mouth.

She wanted to kiss him. She wanted him to leave before he could hurt her even more. Her hands squeezed into fists at her side. "Probably."

Catherine grabbed her shoulder bag. She shot a glance at Kayla before zeroing in on Kane. "You think this is tough, you haven't seen anything yet."

"Goodbye, Catherine." Kayla urged her sister out with her tone of voice.

"I'm going. But you do realize this is getting to be a habit. Him showing up, you kicking me out, him showing up..." Despite Catherine's warning, laughter tinged her voice. Even the tougher Luck sister had a soft spot for Kane McDermott. It didn't bode well for Kayla.

Catherine eased past Kane, slipping beneath his arm and out the door, still muttering aloud the entire time.

"She means well," Kayla said.

"I know. Do you stick up for me the same way when I'm out of earshot?" he asked.

She licked her dry lips, barely able to speak now that they were alone. "A bad habit of mine."

"What is?"

"Sticking up for people I lo..." No. She couldn't lay her heart out for him to trample once more. "What do you want from me, Kane? I made my statement, the captain's filled me in on all I need to know and we said our goodbyes." She nearly choked on the word.

"Well, that's the thing. We didn't—say our goodbyes, that is."

"I don't like games." Not when they hurt her so badly.

"Believe me, sweetheart, this is no game. Think back. You said goodbye, I didn't."

"Is that why you came back? To make sure I knew the score? I'm not stupid, Detective."

His gaze darkened. "I never thought you were."

She knew that. Kane of all people had given her intelligence due respect. Lashing out was the only way she knew to protect herself from what was to come. She just wished she knew exactly what that was.

"I just don't need the word spelled out to know you aren't coming back, that I shouldn't expect anything from you in the future." Her breath caught in her throat and she had to pause for air, until the ability to speak without showcasing her emotions returned. She'd never felt more fragile. "We already covered everything important."

"Not quite everything." He stepped toward her, determined, sexy and sure. Just as he had been the first time, when her life had changed forever.

He grasped her hand and held on tight. He might as well have gripped her heart in his fist. "Did you ever think I didn't say the word goodbye because I didn't mean it?" he asked.

Frustration filled her. She'd had enough of double-talk, word games and drawing out the inevitable pain. "Just like you didn't say I love you because you don't?" She regretted the impulsive, straight-talking words the minute they left her mouth, but once spoken, the truth lay between them.

She tried to jerk her hand free, but he held on with an iron grip. Ignoring his heat was impossible. As always, it elicited an answering liquid warmth inside of her.

She resented the easy hold he had over her, the way he could make her react despite her better judgment. She sighed. "Look, I accepted your limitations, Kane. Now accept mine. You know how I feel about you, so please respect me enough to..."

"Explain?"

"I have a pretty good handle on the whys. I'd rather you just left me alone. It's better for both of us. I know for sure you feel the same way."

"That's what I thought. What I kept telling myself, even as I walked out your front door. But it's not true. I'm a better man with you by my side...and I'd like to think the reverse is true."

His sheepish grin gave rise to spiraling hope deep inside her. Foolish hope. But he had come back. And that was more than she'd ever thought possible.

"And even if you're better off without me, I'm selfish enough to ask you to stay with me anyway."

Kayla's heartbeat tripled and she could barely catch her breath. Kane had never spoken beyond the present before and that was promising. But many other words had been spoken, too.

"What about your edge?" she asked carefully, working hard to bank her hope and her emotions. "You said I distract you…I threaten your ability to be the best cop, the best man, you can be."

"I was wrong. *You* make me be the best I can be." His fingers tightened around hers. "You were right. I've been hanging on to a lot of old guilt, trying to atone with each new case, and making sure I remained miserable in the process."

The future suddenly loomed wide before her, full of possibilities. Full of love. She'd invested all her hopes in this man and he'd come through. She hoped she could repay the gift with a lifetime of love and acceptance.

She glanced at his strained expression, a result of facing his past and baring his soul. For her. "She was your mother. She wouldn't have wanted that, Kane."

He nodded. Kane had told himself the same thing. "I know that now." Reid's unwavering faith in him over the years had finally sunk into his thick skull.

The older man had been right. He'd stopped feeling the day his mother walked in front of that bus. And he hadn't started again until he'd walked in this front door for the first time.

"I haven't given you much reason to believe this, but you're wrong." He looked into liquid green eyes and for the first time let himself hope for the future. "I didn't say I love you—not because I don't, but because I was afraid I didn't deserve you."

"And now?" A pink flush stained her cheeks.

"I still don't deserve you, but I'll be damned if I'll let you go."

"There's that control thing again," she said with a laugh.

Her huge smile eased the tightening in his chest he'd been living with all week. The tightening in other areas, well, Kayla would ease that as well.

"I might let you get away with it this time." She braced her hands on his shoulders. "But you have to say the words, Kane."

He met her gaze head on. "I love you," he said.

She threw herself against his chest, crushing her breasts against him. He inhaled her lemony scent and groaned aloud. "I could get used to this," he said and laughed.

"You'd better, because now that I've got you, I'm not letting you go, either."

"I'm glad to hear that."

Her hands slipped downward and into the back pockets of his old jeans. She gripped him hard in both hands.

"I hope you're thinking what I'm thinking," Kane said. "Because, otherwise, you're playing with fire."

Her soft laugh inflamed his desire. "Want to get Lucky, Detective?"

Those were the last words spoken between them for a good, long while.

Mother's Day is Around the Corner...
Give the gift that celebrates Life and Love!

Show Mom you care by presenting her with a one-year subscription to:

HARLEQUIN WORLD'S BEST Romances

For only $4.96—
That's **75% off the cover price.**

This easy-to-carry, compact magazine delivers 4 exciting romance stories by some of the very best romance authors in the world.

Plus each issue features personal moments with the authors, author biographies, a crossword puzzle and more...

A one-year subscription includes 6 issues full of love, romance and excitement to warm the heart.

To send a gift subscription, write the recipient's name and address on the coupon below, enclose a check for $4.96 and mail it today. In a few weeks, we will send you an acknowledgment letter and a special postcard so you can notify this lucky person that a fabulous gift is on the way!

Back by popular demand are

DEBBIE MACOMBER's

Hard Luck, Alaska, is a
town that needs women!
And the O'Halloran brothers
are just the fellows
to fly them in.

Starting in March 2000 this beloved series returns
in special 2-in-1 collector's editions:

MAIL-ORDER MARRIAGES, featuring
Brides for Brothers and *The Marriage Risk*
On sale March 2000

FAMILY MEN, featuring
Daddy's Little Helper and *Because of the Baby*
On sale July 2000

THE LAST TWO BACHELORS, featuring
Falling for Him and *Ending in Marriage*
On sale August 2000

Collect and enjoy each MIDNIGHT SONS story!

Available at your favorite retail outlet.

HARLEQUIN®
Makes any time special ™

HEART OF THE WEST

Every Man Has His Price!

Lost Springs Ranch was famous for turning young mavericks into good men. So word that the ranch was in financial trouble sent a herd of loyal bachelors stampeding back to Wyoming to put themselves on the auction block!

HARLEQUIN®
Makes any time special ™

Visit us at www.romance.net

PHHOWGEN

HARLEQUIN®

Temptation.

COMING NEXT MONTH

#777 HOT-BLOODED HERO Donna Sterling
Sweet Talkin' Guys

Cole Westcott's marriage to fiery redhead Tess McCrary was *supposed* to be temporary—and strictly platonic. But Tess soon found herself dangerously attracted to her hot-blooded husband. And sweet-talkin' Cole was hard to resist when he suggested that, since they were living together anyway, they might as well share a bed....

#778 ALMOST A COWBOY Ruth Jean Dale
Gone to Texas!

It was "women only" week at the Bar-K Dude Ranch, but Simon Barnett showed up and refused to leave, hollering sexual discrimination. Owner Toni Keene realized the sexy, self-made millionaire was used to getting what he wanted, so she let him stay. Too late, she realized Simon had decided he wanted *her*, too!

#779 SIMPLY SCANDALOUS Carly Phillips
Blaze

Wealthy Assistant D.A. Logan Montgomery needed to ruin his reputation! Otherwise, his father would never give up pushing him into politics. Logan was hoping a very *public* fling with a woman whose family was steeped in scandal would do the trick. But once he met gorgeous Catherine Luck, Logan realized he'd give up everything for one night in Cat's bed....

#780 THE COLORADO KID Vicki Lewis Thompson
Three Cowboys & A Baby

Matty Lang was hopelessly in love with rancher Sebastian Daniels. So she couldn't believe it when she found out a *baby* had been left—on *his* doorstep. Worse, Sebastian thought the little buckaroo was his! There was only one thing to do—seduce Sebastian absolutely senseless. Because no baby girl—or her absentee mother—was going to stop Matty from getting *her* man....

CNM0400